Montgomery Lake High #4

THE BATTLE

FOR INNOCENCE

Written by Stacy A. Padula

Edited by Deb Hartwell

Briley & Baxter Publications | Plymouth, Massachusetts

Paperback ISBN: 978-1-7350168-7-0
Hardcover ISBN: 978-1-7331536-8-3

Book Design: Stacy O'Halloran

*Dedicated to
Marika Adamopoulos*

MEET THE CHARACTERS

Learn more about the characters at www.stacyapadula.com
Follow them on Instagram:
Cathy @ckagelli99
Chantal @chantal_kagelli
Jason @jds_on
Lisa @lisa_ankerman99
Chris @dunkin_85
Alyssa @alyssa_kelly02
The Gripped Series @gripped.book.series

CHAPTER 1

Chantal Kagelli sat silently beside her boyfriend's hospital bed, reflecting on the events of the past month. *Everything is different now,* she thought as she peered at Andy's blank face. *When you wake up, you are going to be so confused. Will you accept that I have rekindled my friendships with Alyssa and Jon? Will you realize the positive impact that your accident has made on our peers? Will you believe that God could transform someone as crude as Jason Davids into a person of integrity and honor? Will you like your new life?*

Chantal gently placed her hand upon Andy's right arm. "Andy, in case you can hear me," she said, "I want to let you know that I miss you. Everyone is thinking about you and praying for you. Jason feels really bad that he didn't run outside to let Lady in during the storm. He thinks that he should be the one in the hospital because Cathy was the one who let Lady outside. I wish you could have seen how many people came to the prayer service that Chris and Jason planned for you. You would have realized how special you are to our school and community.

"You are somehow bringing out the best in people, even while you are in a coma. Chris and Jason planned the prayer service. Afterwards, Jason broke off things with Cathy. As far as I know, he is trying really hard to sober up and better his life. Also, I made up with Alyssa. She realized, finally, that Cathy is manipulative. It turns out that

Alyssa never backstabbed me in seventh grade. Cathy made up that entire story. I cannot believe my sister is such a sociopath. I'm so glad that you two never got close.

"I don't want to overload you, so I'm not going to say much more today," Chantal said, deciding that if Andy could hear her, he would most likely get upset if she mentioned Jon Anderson. "But I want you to know that all of your friends have come together to support each other through this. We are all praying for you and doing our best to be there for your family. I'm going to come visit you again tomorrow. I love you, handsome."

After squeezing Andy's hand, Chantal turned to leave the dimly lit hospital room. As she wandered through the halls of the hospital, she thought back to when she first met Andy in seventh grade. She wondered if he really was *the one*. At that thought, she found her mind wandering to Jon Anderson. Jon had, more so than anyone else, been her rock through this last month of trauma. He was there to encourage her, lift her spirits, and put a smile on her face—he always found a way. Knowing that he was praying for her and knowing that he genuinely cared about her gave Chantal strength.

Realizing that her mind had wandered off Andy, Chantal scolded herself. She felt guilty about valuing Jon's friendship so highly. For the last two years, her life had been comprised of enigmatic situations, entwining Jon, Andy, and her. *In the end, true love will remain,* she reminded herself. *One day, I'll know which boy is right for me.*

When Chantal returned home from the hospital, she dug out a box beneath her bed that was full of old journals. Retrieving a purple one from the box, Chantal stared at its label: Beginning of Seventh Grade. Chantal smiled. *I had no idea what that year had in store…*

CHAPTER 2

Two Years Prior

Chantal Kagelli glanced up at the clock. In twenty-three minutes the bell would ring and she would be set free for the weekend. It was not that Chantal had anything against seventh grade, Sterling Middle School, or her classmates; she was just really excited for her weekend plans.

"Chantal," Andy Rosetti said, tugging on a strand of her auburn hair a few minutes later. Chantal turned around to face her classmate. "What are you doing tonight?" he asked.

"I'm going to youth group with Cathy," Chantal replied, smiling at Andy. "Want to come?"

"Thanks, but no thanks," Andy laughed. "I'm not really into the whole church thing, but I think it's cool that you are."

"That's weird," Chantal sang, eyeing him flirtatiously. "If you think it's cool, then you should get into it."

Andy smiled at Chantal thoughtfully. "Touché, Kagelli. Maybe I'll join you sometime."

"What are *you* doing tonight?" Chantal asked. Her eyes danced as she stared into his light green eyes. Only three weeks into seventh grade, Chantal had found her crush. She knew crushing on Andy was pointless because he did not share her faith, but she couldn't help it; he was captivating.

"My friend Bobby is having people over," Andy replied. "He has a game room in his basement, and his parents let us hangout down there. It's a good time. You should come with me sometime. I think you'd like my friends."

"I'll think about it," Chantal said. "Could I bring my sister? I'm trying to get her to socialize."

"Cathy?" Andy asked, raising his eyebrows.

Chantal nodded.

"Do you think she'd be into hanging out? She seems kind of, I don't know, um—"

"—Boring?"

"You said it not me!" Andy laughed.

Chantal rolled her eyes. "Cathy's not boring; she's just boy-shy. She's actually quite adventurous. She'd kick your butt on the basketball court."

"What! No way! Have you seen me? Have you seen me on the court? I am nasty out there!" Andy exclaimed defensively.

"I think your popularity has gone to your head," Chantal said with a smile. "I'm going to tell her you said that. Maybe you two could play a little one-on-one sometime?"

Andy shook his head and let out a short laugh. "Impossible. It would be a waste of my time."

"Good thing you're cute because you're kind of a jerk," Chantal remarked, standing up from her desk.

"Maybe church would help take the jerk out of me," Andy laughed, sitting on top of his desk.

"If only Montgomery could be so lucky," Chantal sang. In one fluid motion she playfully pushed Andy off of his desk into his chair. Immediately she began running toward the door. Andy recovered from the quick blow to his ego, jumped off his chair, and began chasing after Chantal as the bell rang.

"No running in the classroom!" their teacher scolded.

"Ahhh!" Chantal giggled, realizing that Andy was chasing her out the door.

"I'll chase you all the way to your bus, Kagelli!" Andy called, running after Chantal through the crowded hallway.

"I have to go to my locker," Chantal yelled back, turning the corner to the seventh-grade locker hall.

"Aha, gotcha," Andy proclaimed, pinning Chantal up against her locker. "Have a good weekend," Andy said, smiling and staring her in the eye before walking away.

Chantal let out a heavy breath and stepped away from her locker. Her face was still flushed as she began turning her combination lock.

"That was pretty graphic," Cathy commented, appearing beside Chantal.

"I can't figure him out," Chantal said, sighing with frustration as she opened her locker.

"You and every other girl in our grade," Cathy laughed. "I think he likes you."

Chantal shrugged. "It doesn't matter anyway. Mom and Dad would never let me go out with him."

"You don't think his student council status and elite gym skills could win him some points?" Cathy giggled.

Chantal smirked. "I wish," she said as she shut her locker. "He said he might come to youth group sometime."

"I'm sure not for the right reason," Cathy said. "I think you should forget about Andy, and all of the other boys in your life, and focus on God," she blurted out.

"That's easy for you to say. You don't even like boys!" Chantal exclaimed.

Cathy crossed her arms. "I like boys," she retorted. "I just like other things, too. Don't you think God has the perfect guy for you?"

"To marry, I guess," Chantal replied, shrugging as she walked away from her locker. "Too bad the only cute boy in youth group moved away. I really thought we had potential."

Cathy rolled her eyes. "Shocking."

Chantal shrugged. "Well, what can I expect from a sixth-grade crush? He didn't even say goodbye."

"Maybe he hates you," Cathy suggested with amusement.

"Thanks a lot," Chantal said, pushing Cathy in the shoulder.

CHAPTER 3

"Dude, you're going to miss out," Jason's voice rang through the telephone into Jon's ear on Friday afternoon.

"Nah, I think you're missing out," Jon said, unzipping his suitcase.

"So, let me get this straight," Jason continued. "You just got back from California, you haven't seen the crew in two weeks, Chris's parents are away, Taylor lets us do whatever we want, and you're going to church?"

"And you're the one missing out," Jon finished, tossing dirty clothes out of his suitcase.

"You're tapped!" Jason laughed.

"I'll see you guys at Sartelli's tomorrow," Jon said, disregarding Jason's mockery. "Kick-off's at one?"

"Dude, you're so lame!" Jason whined. "Taylor is buying the fight. Luke, Matt, Samson, and all those guys are going. Chris even invited some girls."

"Not girls I'm interested in," Jon replied carelessly.

"Alyssa's going," Jason said, referring to Jon's best friend.

"Is she?" Jon asked. "I haven't even talked to her since I got back. She'll have a good time with you guys. I think she and Sartelli should get together."

"Nah, he's all hung up on that girl from his school," Jason replied.

"That'll pass," Jon predicted.

"He won't even invite her to hang out with us," Jason said. "I don't know what that's all about."

"I do," Jon said with a laugh. "You and Chris are the last people I'd introduce a girl I like to. Girls either hate you or love you. There's no in between."

"Ah, that classic fine line," Jason retorted. "Dude, I can't wait for high school. My day at Saint T's consists of a bunch of dudes and religion being shoved down my throat. Sounds like your type of place, Anderson."

"Since I like boys and all," Jon said sarcastically.

"So, you're seriously not coming to Chris's tonight?" Jason questioned him in disbelief. "Alyssa's bringing friends."

"Jay, I see those girls every day at school," Jon retorted. "They're no big deal to me."

"I swear you're a homo dude," Jason ragged. "A hundred bucks says I lose my virginity before you even kiss a girl."

"The girl I kiss will be worth more than your girl's virginity and a hundred bucks combined," Jon stated confidently.

"Wow, someone's high on himself," Jason remarked. "You sound like you have someone in mind."

"I have seven years of prayer invested in this girl," Jon said. "When God opens my eyes to see who she is, I will spend the rest of my life loving her. You might have sex binding you guys together, but we'll have Christ. You think I'm crazy, but I know what a relationship looks like when Christ is in the center of it. I'm not settling for anything less than that."

"You're so full of it," Jason laughed. "You'll get drunk and lose it to Alyssa before you turn sixteen. I can appreciate high standards, but be realistic, Anderson."

"That's disgusting," Jon groaned. "If that's your prediction, keep me away from alcohol."

"Ha!" Jason cackled. "Keeping you away from alcohol won't be hard if you keep ditching us for church."

"There's a girl there who I think you'd like," Jon said.

"Yeah, I don't think so," Jason shot back.

"I have to go," Jon said suddenly, glancing at the clock.

"Praise the Lord!" Jason mocked in a loud squeaky tone.

Jon rolled his eyes and hung up the phone. He knew Jason meant well but had a terrible way of showing it. Jon feared that Jason's negative attitude toward religion would someday drive a wedge into their friendship. Jason and his two older brothers had gone to Catholic elementary school. Unlike Jason, Luke and Matt Davids had been allowed to attend Hamilton Middle School. Jason's parents had always favored Jason; as a result, they wanted him to study at a prestigious school until college. Their idea had shattered Jon, Jason, Chris, and Bryan's childhood dream of being united at Montgomery Lake High.

Jason, being as persuasive as usual, had talked his parents into making a compromise: he would be allowed to attend MLH if he made high honors every term at St. Timothy's. Since St. Timothy's had a reputation for being one of the toughest schools in Massachusetts, it did not seem like Jason's parents had made much of a compromise. Jon knew that they had; Jason was a genius. In less than two years Jon, Jason, Chris, and Bryan would begin living their childhood dream under the roof of MLH.

Jon opened his carry-on bag and pulled his Bible out of it. He was opening to the Gospel of Mark when his phone began ringing. "Hello," he called into it, hoping it would be for his mother so he could read before youth group.

"Hey, dude, what's up?" Chris Dunkin's voice drilled through Jon's ear.

Jon sighed. "Hey, what's up, man?"

"Tell me the rumor's not true!" Chris laughed. "Are you really bailing on us tonight?"

"I'll see you guys tomorrow at Sartelli's," Jon replied, sounding more frustrated than he had meant to.

"All right, guy, fair enough," Chris complied with ease. "Looking forward to it."

"So, what's the deal at your house tonight? Who's going?" Jon asked, closing his Bible.

"It's nothing special," Chris said. "Taylor, Jordan, and Marc invited some people over to watch the fight."

"Nice. Well, have fun," Jon remarked, glancing at the clock again. "I have to jet."

"All right, man. Have a good night at church," Chris said without ridicule. "You can stop by later if you feel like crashing here."

"Thanks. I'll talk to my mom," Jon replied.

After hanging up the phone, Jon pondered over asking if he could sleep at Chris's. The last time Chris's cousin Taylor babysat, he threw a rager that caught the attention of seventy-five percent of

Montgomery's police force. Jon wanted no part of that type of gathering. Although Jon was a fan of Marc Dunkin, Taylor's youngest brother, he thought Mr. and Mrs. Dunkin were crazy to leave their children in their nephews' care. Taylor was a junior in college, Jordan was a senior at MLH, and Marc was a sophomore at MLH; not one of them was a suitable role model for Chris or his nine-year-old sister, Katie.

Chris had always been an unintentional troublemaker. Jon thought that recently Chris had become a more intentional one. Whether it was a result of Taylor's influence, Chris's parents' frequent travels, or both, Jon could not decide. Chris was the best friend Jon could have ever asked for, and he hated the thought of Chris getting mixed up in his cousin's lifestyle. Part of Jon wanted to go to Chris's—just to check up on him—and part of him wanted to avoid the scene all together.

"Jon!" his mother called from downstairs. "We have to leave in two minutes!"

"Okay, thanks!" Jon hollered back, hoping Pastor Mark's teaching at youth group would enlighten him on how to deal with his friends.

Chantal was unusually quiet on the ride to youth group. Her mother and Cathy were enjoying light conversation in the front seat, while Chantal sat analyzing herself in silence. Was she excited for youth group because of the boys that paid her attention? She hoped she was excited to study the Bible, but feared she was more excited about the boys.

"Have fun. I'll see you guys at nine," Mrs. Kagelli said, pulling the car up to the front door of the church.

"Bye, Mom," Chantal called while hopping out of the back seat. "Love you!"

"Thanks for the ride. Love you!" Cathy said, kissing her mother on the cheek before exiting the car. "I always get nervous coming here," Cathy admitted to Chantal as they walked into the church.

"To church?" Chantal asked, raising her eyebrows in confusion.

"No, to youth group," Cathy clarified. "I hate how easy it is for you to socialize. Am I that much of a dork that people are completely disinterested?"

Chantal laughed. "You're not a dork! You're way cooler than I am. People are probably more interested in getting to know you than me. I'm an open book. I wear my heart on my sleeve. You are *mysterious*."

Cathy rolled her green eyes and smiled. "Thanks, Chantal."

"Hi, Cathy! Hi, Chantal!" Jessie Robins greeted them near the youth group's meeting room.

"Hi!" Cathy called, waving and smiling warmly.

"Jessie, I love your shirt!" Chantal exclaimed, rushing to Jessie's side. "Is it new?"

"Actually, it's Sarah's," Jessie replied and began walking with the twins into the meeting room.

"Oh, I want to borrow it sometime. She has good—" Chantal's words dissolved in her mouth as she stepped through the door.

"Good taste?" Jessie asked, pausing at Chantal's side.

"Oh!" Cathy yelped, stumbling into Jessie as her eyes followed Chantal's gaze and landed upon Jon Anderson.

"Yeah, really good taste," Chantal recovered, dropping her eyes to the floor and hustling to the first available seat.

"I thought we were going to sit together," Cathy whispered as she and Jessie walked past Chantal. They sat down in the next available seats, which were ten feet away from Chantal.

"Is there room for me down there?" Chantal asked after snapping out of shock.

"I'll be getting up to sing in a minute. You can take my seat," Jessie offered. "Just squeeze between Cathy and me for now."

"Thanks," Chantal said, rushing over to the girls. As Chantal sat down between the girls—and behind Jon—she was certain her face matched the red tone of her hair.

"Hi, Cathy," Jon greeted her, turning around in his chair.

"Hi," Cathy replied softly, making eye contact with him for a split second.

"Hi, Chantal, hi Jessie, hi Sarah," Jon said, peeling his brown eyes off Cathy.

"What are you doing here?" Chantal asked flatly.

Jon raised his eyebrows. "Um, it should be pretty obvious."

"She means, why aren't you in California?" Cathy clarified.

"Oh!" Jon said with a laugh. "I flew home today. I thought you might have heard about my best friend's party tonight or something."

Chantal glanced at Cathy strangely.

"Didn't you tell me that you were going to stay with your dad in California for a while?" Cathy asked. "As in, moving there?"

"What?" Jon laughed. "No!"

Chantal turned completely pale.

"Wow, I really misunderstood you," Cathy said, widening her bright green eyes.

"Don't you think I would have said bye if I was *moving* away?" Jon asked, glancing at Chantal.

Chantal shrugged. "It's not like we hang out."

"Well, maybe we should change that in case I move." Jon laughed. "Then I'd have an excuse to say goodbye."

Chantal smiled slightly.

"So, who's your best friend?" Cathy asked, cocking her head to the side. "And what kind of party is he having?"

"Oh, my friend Chris from school," Jon replied. "He's not having the type of party I'd want to attend."

"Chris Dunkin," Jessie chimed in. "We're in a few classes together. I heard him announce it today in English."

"Really? Did he invite a lot of people?" Jon asked, looking as though Jessie's words had caught him off guard.

"I think everyone except me," Jessie replied. "So, that should answer your question, Cathy."

"They're the ones missing out," Jon said and winked at Jessie.

Jessie smiled. "I agree."

As Jessie stood up to join the worship team in the front of the room, Chantal bowed her head in prayer. *Dear God, what is going on? Just when my eyes are open to see that I have made boys idols in my heart, Jon comes back into the picture. I like him so much. Please drain the feelings I have for him out of my heart. I don't want to like him. I want my heart to be purely for You. Please help me focus on You tonight. Please guard my mind from thoughts of Jon. Please, please, please drain my heart of feelings for Jon. Please help me. I want You to be all that I want. I pray this all in Jesus' name. Amen.*

"Holy fire… burn away… my desire… for anything… that is not of You… and is of me… I want more of You… and less of me," Jessie began singing a moment later.

Perfect, Chantal thought as she quietly sang along.

CHAPTER 4

Pastor Mark was teaching on Ephesians 5:1-20. Jon sat in silence, taking in all of Pastor Mark's words. It seemed as though God was using Pastor Mark as a mouthpiece to speak directly to Jon's heart. Jon thought God might have been showing him that he was called to be separate. Although staying friends with Chris, Jason, and Bryan was important, Jon knew staying in step with God was much more imperative. If he wanted to continue to grow in his walk with Christ, he needed to have nothing to do with "unfruitful works of darkness." That was exactly what he thought of Taylor Dunkin's parties. *What good came from them? Temporary pleasure and a long list of consequences?* Jon knew that his time should be spent "making the most of every opportunity" and finding out what God wanted him to do.

After Pastor Mark's message was over, Jon thought God could be leading him to spend less time with Chris, Jason, and Bryan. Honestly, he dreaded the thought. He believed God's Word; he believed that God withheld no good thing from those who walked uprightly; he believed that God knew what was best for his future. Even so, the idea of distancing himself from his friends grieved his heart. *Who would I hang out with? Who would have my back? How could I hurt the guys who have always been there for me? Shouldn't I be a light in their world? Aren't I supposed to be a light in dark places? Am I a good influence on them, or are they bad influences on me?* Jon's mind was filled with questions, and his heart was deeply troubled.

"How's it going, Jon?" Chantal asked, walking over to him with Cathy.

"Would you guys mind praying with me about something?" Jon asked, glancing from Chantal to Cathy.

"Sure," Chantal shrugged, taking a seat beside Jon.

"I get really nervous praying out loud," Cathy admitted, sitting down next to Chantal, "but I'll definitely pray with you."

"Awesome guys, thanks," Jon said and smiled. "I'm just worried about some of my friends that are at Chris's party. There are some people there who could be bad influences on them. I don't want them to get pulled into that scene. Chris's older cousin is housesitting, and he's really not, um, how do I say this?" Jon stammered. "He's really engulfed in darkness."

"What kind of darkness?" Cathy asked curiously.

"I'd rather keep it vague," Jon said, glancing at Cathy. "But honestly, I'm curious, too. I really have no idea what they're up to. One of my friends called and made it sound like Chris's party was a huge deal. Then Chris called and said it was nothing special. I thought my first friend was just trying to talk it up, but when Jessie said Chris invited her entire English class it made me think Chris had mislead me."

"Well, maybe he really doesn't think it's a big deal," Chantal suggested. "Maybe he meant it wasn't anything special to your standards. Does Chris support your faith?"

"He's not opposed to it like some of the other guys," Jon replied. "He respects my beliefs. He's a good friend."

"Then it's probably just Satan trying to get you to doubt Chris's sincerity," Chantal reasoned. "If Satan gets you to doubt your friends' loyalty then you'll be less apt to pray for them. You know?"

Jon cocked his head to the side. "Chantal, I'm sorry, I just didn't realize you had so much wisdom," he said.

Chantal blushed and looked away from Jon.

"So, I'd really like it if we could pray for Chris and everyone else at his party," Jon said. "I haven't seen them in a couple of weeks, and I'm worried about them."

"Okay, you start," Chantal said, nodding slightly in Jon's direction.

"Father, I thank you that you have blessed me with friends to pray with. Thank you for youth group and Pastor Mark's message tonight. You always know exactly how to meet me where I'm at. I lift

Chris up to you, and I thank you for his friendship. Please help me be a light in his life. Please put more lights in his life that will draw him to You. Please protect Alyssa, Jason, and Bryan tonight. Please help me stay strong in You. Help me flee from temptation. Please put friends in my life that will hold me accountable. It's so hard sometimes to be the only Christian in my circle of friends. I don't want to give up on them, but I don't want them to drag me away from You. Show me what to do. Thank you for listening to my prayers and for bringing me here tonight. In Jesus' name, Amen," Jon prayed.

"Dear Lord, I lift Jon's friends up to you. If there is anything illegal going on at the party, please send the police to Chris's house. I pray that Jon's friends will welcome you into their lives. Please continue to lay them on my heart to pray for. Thank you for opening my eyes to see You at such a young age. Help me to stay on the path you have designed for my life. I pray this all in Jesus' name. Amen," Chantal prayed softly.

"Amen," Cathy and Jon said in unison.

"Thank you so much," Jon expressed with sincere gratitude. "As you can probably tell, the message really hit home with me tonight."

"Me, too," Chantal nodded. "It helped me put some things into perspective. Although, Cathy is pretty good at doing that, too."

"I always thought it would be the coolest thing to have an identical twin," Jon smiled. "What do you think Cathy? Why are you so quiet all the time?"

Cathy shrugged and smiled innocently. "Oh, I don't know. I guess I'm a better listener than speaker."

"I don't know about that," Jon said, eyeing her skeptically. "I think you just haven't come out of your shell."

"Maybe," Cathy sang. "I'm not quiet on the soccer field or the basketball court. That's for sure."

"Yeah, Cathy's actually not shy at all, once you get to know her," Chantal commented, smiling at her sister. "She's good at putting me in my place."

Jon laughed. "I wish just one of my best friends would become a Christian," he said earnestly. "I know you guys don't know him, but Chris is an awesome kid. Everyone loves him. He always has a fun idea up his sleeve. Once he has your back, everyone leaves you alone. Seriously, Chris is the coolest kid in my school. He dominates the baseball and football fields. None of us can keep up with him. I wish he'd come to church with me."

"Does he believe in God?" Cathy asked.

"He says he does, but his actions don't line up with his words," Jon shrugged. "I'm just afraid he's getting into bad things. I hope not, but I feel like he's keeping things from me. Well… he *did* invite me to crash at his house tonight, so I don't think he's trying to hide anything *too* big from me."

"Are you going there?" Chantal asked with confusion written all over her face.

"After Pastor Mark's message?" Jon asked. "Absolutely!"

Chantal raised her eyebrows at Jon.

"No way," Jon laughed, shaking his head.

"Yeah, I didn't think so," Chantal giggled.

"It's almost nine!" Cathy announced suddenly. "Mom is probably waiting outside. We should go."

"Okay," Chantal said, jumping up from her seat. "It was awesome praying with you, Jon. I'll keep your friends in my prayers this week."

"Thanks," Jon said. "Maybe I'll see you guys on Sunday."

"Bye," Cathy called, heading toward the exit.

"Bye," Jon said, smiling brightly at Chantal as she walked out the door backwards.

CHAPTER 5

"Jon didn't move to California!" Cathy exclaimed as soon as she hopped into her mother's car.

Mrs. Kagelli turned to face Cathy in the backseat. "You sound awfully excited," she said, gazing at her suspiciously.

Cathy shrugged. "I just think he's awesome. All of his friends are at a party tonight, but he still came to youth group. He's the only guy that seems like he is actually there for the lesson and not the socializing."

"He was nice to me," Chantal informed her mother as she put on her seatbelt. "When I first saw him, I felt so awkward."

"Why?" Mrs. Kagelli asked, steering the car out of the church parking lot.

"He must know that I've been obsessed with him since sixth grade!" Chantal cried. "That is really embarrassing. He's completely uninterested in girls. He must think I'm a horrible Christian."

"Having interest in a boy does not make you a horrible Christian," her mother laughed. "It makes you a normal thirteen-year-old girl. God puts desires in your heart, you know. Your attraction to Jon could very well be from God."

"Obviously it's not!" Chantal exclaimed. "It would be mutual if it was from God. I don't trust my heart. It lies to me all the time. I just want the feelings taken away."

"You should pray about the feelings instead of just praying for them to be removed," her mother advised. "What if God is trying to point Jon out to you? You don't want to be blind to whatever God is trying to show you because you are fearful. It's not wise to assume having feelings for Jon is a bad thing. Pray about your feelings and see what God reveals to you."

"He's going to show me that I am boy-crazy," Chantal remarked, glancing out the window.

"Now, if you were talking about your feelings for Andy, I would give you different advice," Mrs. Kagelli continued.

"Well, that's completely different," Chantal stated, turning toward her mother.

"How is it different?" Mrs. Kagelli asked.

"I shouldn't want to go out with someone who doesn't share my faith," Chantal replied. "I'm attracted to Andy's looks and personality, but I know he is not good for me."

"Didn't you just say that liking Jon is wrong, too?" Mrs. Kagelli questioned her, raising her eyebrows.

"Ye-ah…but…it's wrong for different reasons," Chantal said slowly. "It's wrong because Jesus should be enough for me. I shouldn't want to date anyone. I want God to be my only desire. I hate how much I like boys."

Mrs. Kagelli laughed. "Chantal, I've had a crush on your father since I was seven years old! He didn't notice me until our senior year of high school. After being married for fifteen years, I can tell you that the crush was put there for a reason. It was not sinful for me to have interest in your father. If I didn't, then you would not exist!"

Chantal frowned. "So, it's not wrong for me to like Jon?"

"Pray about it, and see what God shows you," Mrs. Kagelli replied. "If the feelings are not from God, He will cleanse your heart—if you genuinely want Him to. If your heart's desire is to honor God with your relationships, then He will align your heart with His will. Praying isn't about begging God for the things we want; it's about Him aligning our hearts with His desires for us."

CHAPTER 6

The next afternoon, Jon walked into Bryan's house, eager for the scheduled football scrimmage. Bryan lived in one of the largest developments in Montgomery, so his house was the boys' prime meeting spot for sporting events. The last time Jon played, he had not been on Chris's team and therefore had not tasted victory. Jon was eager to get a second chance at humbling his best friend.

"What's going on, dudes?" Jon greeted Bryan and Jason as he walked into the living room. They were lifelessly lying on separate couches, watching TV.

"Hey, man. What's up?" Bryan muttered.

"Where's Chris?" Jon asked, sitting down beside Bryan. "I figured he'd be the first one here, raring to get out on the field."

Jason let out a short laugh. Bryan picked a pillow up off the couch and threw it at Jason. "Chris is up to his eye sockets in debris right now," Bryan stated with a laugh.

Jon glanced from Bryan to Jason. "What went down last night?"

"Dude, I told you that you were going to miss out," Jason said with a smirk. "There had to have been at least fifty people crammed into his house."

"More than that!" Bryan exclaimed, widening his eyes. "You missed a bunch of stuff when you went upstairs, dude. People were coming and going all night."

"So, you guys got to be flies on a wall at a college party?" Jon asked.

"A college party with a lot of hot high school girls," Jason laughed. "Matt's girlfriend, Laurelle, was there with her friends. They're all Varsity cheerleaders. Oh my gosh dude. Hot. Yeah, real hot."

"They probably felt like their little brothers were watching them get wasted," Jon stated. "Didn't you feel out of place?"

"I think Jay got more comfortable than anyone," Bryan snickered.

"Oh, I forgot to tell you," Jason sang. "You owe me a hundred bucks."

Jon stared at Jason blankly for a few seconds, and then slowly dropped his jaw.

Jason nodded. "That's right."

"Who?" Jon asked, widening his eyes with curiosity.

Jason smiled. "The hottest girl at MLH's little sister."

"She goes to my school," Bryan chimed in. "She's in eighth grade."

"How does that just happen?" Jon asked, sounding distraught.

Jason laughed. "Four letters. Two are the same. The word begins with a 'b'. You're up Jonny-boy!"

"You got her drunk?" Jon asked, eyeing Jason uneasily.

"Oh, he didn't have to," Bryan chuckled. "She was on him the second he walked through the door. Matt made an announcement that Jay was a big deal and the rest was history."

"Do you like this girl?" Jon questioned him.

"I don't know her," Jason replied, "so how could I like her? Do I like her body? Yes, very much."

"Are you going to see her again?" Jon asked.

"Hopefully," Jason shrugged. "I think Taylor's going to throw another party. Jordan has a thing for her sister. He's trying to nail her, but I guess she's pretty hard to get."

"The hottest girl at MLH?" Jon asked. "That should be obvious. She wouldn't be considered the hottest girl if she gave herself away."

"True," Jason agreed. "Well, I think her sister is sick of living in her shadow. She basically dragged me up to Chris's room."

"Does she have a name?" Jon asked. "Or does it make you feel better to call her the *hottest girl* at MLH's sister?"

"Ha," Jason laughed. "Her name's Kristen."

Jon stared at Jason, unsure of how to react. Should he congratulate him? Congratulating someone for losing his virginity did not line up with Jon's profession of faith. He knew Jason was anxious for Jon's response; he would call Jon a hypocrite if he congratulated him and a prude if he reprimanded him. "How was your night, Bry-guy?" Jon asked, trying to change the subject.

"I basically chilled all night with Chris, Alyssa, and the friends she brought," Bryan said with a shrug. "They're a good time. We watched the fight, played some drinking games, and took a bunch of pictures."

"You guys drank?" Jon asked, hating everything he had heard so far about Chris's party.

"I didn't," Jason said. "Matt would rip me a new one if I started pounding beers in front of him. Somehow, I lost my virginity before I ever got drunk. I didn't think it would happen that way, but I'm not complaining."

"Did Taylor let Chris drink?" Jon asked.

"I think Taylor's logic is if he can get Chris to do what he does, then Chris won't tell on him," Bryan said.

Jason laughed. "He's right."

"Taylor does a lot of crap!" Jon exclaimed, horrified by Bryan's theory.

"You act like it's a bad thing," Jason retorted. "Taylor can't make Chris do anything he doesn't want to do. I don't think he'd ever force him into anything. I think Marc would prevent that from happening. He's protective of Chris."

"Marc's the man, but I could take or leave his brothers," Jon stated disapprovingly. "So, last night, you lost your virginity, Chris got wasted, and Jordan tried to nail the hottest girl at MLH but failed. Did anything else happen that's worth talking about?"

"Alyssa's friends were cute," Bryan commented. "I think Chris was kind of into one of them."

"Who'd she bring?" Jon asked.

"Some girl Leslie, and this girl Katherine, and another girl named Lisa," Bryan said. "They were all hot. One of them—Lisa—wow!"

"Leslie Lucus and Katherine Rossi?" Jon asked.

Bryan shrugged. "We didn't get into last names. You must know them, dude. They're the girls you and Chris hang out with at school."

"I don't know anyone named Lisa," Jon said. "Leslie and Katherine are cool. They're tamer than Alyssa, so I'm surprised they went."

"Only Lisa played the drinking game with Chris and me. The other three girls just watched," Bryan explained. "Actually, we kind of paired off. Alyssa and I were a team, Chris and Leslie were a team, and Lisa and Katherine were a team. We drank for our sober teammates."

"Who was Chris into?" Jon asked curiously.

"He thought Lisa was hot," Bryan stated flatly.

"He wants her," Jason chimed in.

"What school is she from?" Jon asked.

"Sterling," Bryan replied.

"I have friends who go there," Jon said, thinking of Cathy and Chantal.

"Friends from church?" Jason asked.

"Yup," Jon replied, anticipating a mocking blow in his direction.

"Girls?" Jason pressed.

"*Twin* girls," Jon nodded.

"Ooooh," Jason sang, lowering his eyebrows, "that sounds kind of hot, Anderson. No wonder you've been skipping out on us for youth group. You're working two girls at once."

Jon laughed. "I don't even know how to respond to that."

"Oh, the cops came," Bryan added. "I was already passed out, but Chris told me this morning. I guess they broke the party up around two. No one got arrested, but people had to leave."

At the sound of Bryan's words, Jon remembered Chantal's prayer. He became more worried about Chris than ever. Mr. and Mrs. Dunkin were not due back to Montgomery for a week. He wondered how many more parties Taylor had marked on the calendar.

"Oh, by the way, football's cancelled," Bryan said. "Chris is going to be cleaning all day, I'm wicked tired, and Jay's a little sore."

"Screw you!" Jason exclaimed, whipping the remote control at Bryan. Bryan caught the remote and laughed. Jon rolled his eyes, despising how lightly his friends took the subject of pre-marital sex. Hearing that Jason had lost his virginity to someone he did not even love appalled Jon. Jon knew Jason would mistreat Kristen. Even if they dated, Jason would not respect her. He was used to girls throwing themselves at him, just like she had.

Despite the fact that Jason went to an all-boys private school, he was well known around Montgomery for his beauty and brains. Jason did not have to treat a girl with respect to get her respect. He could pretty much do anything, and girls would still fight over him. Girls tended to have the same type of reaction over Chris. Chris had the muscles, the charisma, and the smile that drew everyone in. Jon knew that was why Bryan abstained from inviting the girl he liked to hang out with them. He astutely feared losing her to Jason or Chris. Jon wouldn't put it past either of them to scoop her up, even though they knew Bryan liked her. Sadly, all of Jon's friends were ruthlessly competitive with each other, especially when it came to girls.

CHAPTER 7

One Week Later

Dear God,
I have been praying now for about six months that You would take away my feelings for Jon. What is this unquenchable burden on my heart? It scares me. I don't want to like Jon. I don't want to like anyone. I want to be content being single. Please drain my heart of my own desires and fill my heart with Your desires. My mom said I should pray about why Jon is in my heart, but I'm scared. I'm afraid I will get more attached if I start praying about him. I'd like to just fight these feelings off, but I can't in my own strength. Please help me. I pray this all in Jesus' name. Amen.
Love,
Chantal

Sunday morning, Chantal was walking her younger sister, Stephanie, to the Sunday School classroom when she saw Jon talking to Cathy. A vibe of panic shot through her body, sending her heart into rapid beats. Jon was smiling, Cathy was laughing, and Chantal was turning pale. There was something about the way Cathy and Jon were leaning into each other that caused the color to drain from Chantal's face. Glancing at the bright smile on Cathy's face, Chantal realized what had set off her internal alarm. Cathy looked more than interested in the conversation; she looked interested in Jon!

CHAPTER 8

“Hi, is Alyssa there?” Jon spoke into his cordless phone Sunday afternoon. He fell back on his bed and waited for Alyssa to come to the phone.

“Hi, Jon!” Alyssa’s voice squeaked thirty seconds later.

Jon laughed. “I must call you too often if your mom recognized my voice.”

“Caller ID, buddy,” Alyssa giggled.

“Oh, all right. Then I guess I can still call you,” Jon replied in an amused manner.

“So, what’s up?” Alyssa asked.

“I wanted to talk about the friend you brought to Chris’s last weekend,” Jon said.

“Lisa?” Alyssa asked.

“Yeah, I heard she was a hit,” Jon emphasized. “Chris mentioned her to me a few times.”

“Me, too,” Alyssa said. “I think she’s interested in him. I told Chris that. He said he might be able to have another party in a few weeks, when his parents go to Florida.”

Jon sighed.

“What do you want to know about Lisa?” Alyssa asked.

“She goes to Sterling, right?”

“Yeah.”

“Do you know if she knows the Kagelli twins?”

"I can find out," Alyssa offered. "Why? Who are they?"

"Some girls I go to church with," Jon replied. "I'm kind of curious about them."

"Interested or curious?" Alyssa pressed, sounding intrigued.

"You know me, Lyss," Jon sang. "Just curious."

"Jason said you're acting like you're interested in someone," Alyssa stated. "Is he talking out of his butt like usual, or is there something to his theory?"

Jon laughed. "Jason's words are unreliable."

"You *would* say that. Well, I'll ask Lisa about them," Alyssa agreed. "She seems pretty social, so she probably knows them."

"How do you know her anyway?" Jon asked.

"She cheers with Leslie and Katherine," Alyssa replied. "I invited them to Chris's, but they already had plans with Lisa. It worked out well that she came. We've been messaging each other all week. She seems wicked cool."

"Hey, it never hurts to bring around a pretty face," Jon laughed.

"I wish you never said that Bryan and I would be cute together," Alyssa said. "I keep thinking about the possibility, and I'm starting to like him. Don't you dare tell him I said that."

"Well, I never should have said that to you," Jon admitted. "Jason thinks Bryan is still interested in that girl from his school. I told him that it will pass, but Bryan seems pretty into her."

"Is he hooking up with her?" Alyssa asked.

"I have no idea," Jon replied. "He's really quiet about that type of thing."

"Then why do you think we'd be good together?" Alyssa pressed.

"I just think your personalities click well," Jon said. "You're always up for a good time, and he's chill like that."

"He and Chris were drinking at the party," Alyssa said disapprovingly.

"I heard," Jon stated flatly.

"It was weird," Alyssa admitted. "I think we're kind of young for that. Jordan dropped two beers in front of them and said, 'pound these.' He would have done the same to Jason if Matt weren't there. Matt seemed pretty pissed that kids in middle school were drinking. I don't even think he and Luke were drinking."

"Matt's pretty tame," Jon said. "I hope Jason follows his path."

"Jay's a *much* bigger jerk than Matt or Luke Davids," Alyssa expressed emphatically.

"True," Jon agreed. "I was glad you, Leslie, and Katherine didn't drink."

"Oh, we wouldn't," Alyssa assured him. "Katherine was pretty horrified by the way the older kids were acting. I doubt she'll come to Chris's again."

"I don't really know Katherine well, but she seems a little too quiet for Chris's house," Jon reasoned.

"I think *I* might be a little too quiet for Chris's house these days," Alyssa said with a laugh.

"I'm heading over there in a few to watch the game," Jon said. "I'm hoping it will just be us so I can talk to him about things. He worries me."

"Tell him not to smoke anymore. He's going to get addicted," Alyssa said. "Tell him Lisa doesn't like guys who smoke."

Jon's heart began pounding against his chest. "He was smoking? Are you serious?"

"I thought you knew that," Alyssa replied. "He said he's been smoking since the summer. He claims it's not a habit, but it looked that way to me. Actually, Bryan was smoking, too. It was weird."

"What is going on?!" Jon exclaimed. "Jay, too?"

"No, Jason gave them crap for it," Alyssa stated. "He thinks smoking is lame and unattractive."

"It is," Jon agreed. "Marc must have freaked out."

"I don't think he noticed," Alyssa said. "He was preoccupied with trying to keep his brother away from one of his friends. I guess Jordan has a thing for one of the girls Marc hangs out with."

"The hottest girl at MLH?" Jon asked.

"She's pretty," Alyssa replied.

"I heard about that," Jon said. "Marc's of a whole different breed than the rest of the Dunkins. I bet he wasn't drinking either."

"None of the football players were supposed to drink," Alyssa said. "They had a game the next day."

"Isn't Jordan the captain?" Jon asked.

"Well, it's like you said; Marc is of a complete different breed than his brothers," Alyssa said matter-of-factly.

"All right, well, I have to head over to Chris's," Jon sighed. "Thanks for letting me know all this stuff. Let me know what Lisa says about the Kagellis."

"You've got me curious about these girls," Alyssa laughed. "They must be something special to stir up your interest."

"My curiosity, not interest," Jon corrected her.

"Oh, right," Alyssa said. "Peace out, lover boy. Go lay some sense into Chris."

"Bye Lyss," Jon sang, hanging up the phone. He sat on his bed for a moment, collecting his thoughts. It seemed like the more he prayed for his friends the worse off they became. Or was it that the more he prayed, the more he found out? That seemed more like it. After all, he had prayed for hidden things to come to the light. Everything that was coming to the light was horrifying him.

Chris had always been focused on athletics and physical fitness, so why would he start drinking and smoking? If Chris took a turn down a bad road, then many others were sure to follow him without question. Chris was the leader of their clique and one of the most influential kids at Montgomery Lake Middle School.

CHAPTER 9

After church, Chantal tucked herself away in her bedroom. Cathy had said nothing about Jon on the ride home from church, which made Chantal more suspicious. She thought of asking Cathy if she had feelings for Jon. Chantal went back and forth debating if knowing the truth would be a good thing. If Cathy liked Jon, then would Chantal have to ignore her own feelings to honor her sister? Would the twins have to compete for his adoration? That would be divisively dreadful.

"Okay, Lord," Chantal sighed, grabbing her Bible off her nightstand, "what do You want to tell me about my feelings for Jon?" She flipped open the Bible randomly and glanced down at the page with curiosity. She had opened to 2 Corinthians 12. "The vision of paradise," she smiled, skimming the first part of the passage. "I like that!" After reading a few verses about the apostle Paul being caught up into the third heaven, Chantal made no connection to her feelings for Jon. She continued reading. "The thorn in the flesh," she said slowly.

As her eyes skimmed verse eight, Chantal's heart leaped within her chest. "I pleaded with the Lord three times that it might depart from me. And He said to me, 'My grace is sufficient for you, for My strength is made perfect in weakness,'" she read, staring at the Bible in awe. "Oh my gosh," she whispered, letting out a heavy breath. "Therefore most gladly I will rather boast in my infirmities, that the power of Christ may rest upon me. Therefore I take pleasures in infirmities, in reproaches, in needs, in persecutions, in distresses, for Christ's sake. For when I am weak, then I am strong," she read quickly.

Chantal pushed the Bible off her lap and fell to her knees. "Father, forgive me," she said. "Paul, whom I admire so much, pleaded with You only three times for his burden to be removed. I have pleaded with You hundreds of times, refusing to accept that this could be from You. Your strength is made perfect in *my* weakness. Jon is *definitely* one of my weaknesses. I cannot fight off these feelings. I have tried with all my strength. I think that is why I even allowed myself to entertain thoughts of Andy. I hoped they would suppress my heartache for Jon. Oh please forgive me, Father," Chantal pleaded. "Help me to allow You to be glorified through my weaknesses. Help me to step aside and let You work. Help me to understand that Your grace is sufficient. Please give me Your strength so I can take this situation to prayer, as my mother suggested. I have let fear hinder me from praying about Jon so many times. I know fear and faith cannot coexist. Forgive me for my lack of faith. Forgive me for housing fear, unbelief, and worry in my heart. Oh Lord, I have approached this whole thing from such a warped perspective. Help me to see this through Your eyes. Help me to see Jon the way You want me to see Him. Please align our hearts with Your will. Please bind all the spirits of fear that are oppressing me. If You are allowing this thorn to remain in my flesh then I know it must serve a purpose. Please help me to trust You more. I pray this in Jesus' name. Amen."

Chantal arose from the floor and flopped onto her bed. "There are over twenty-five hundred pages in my study Bible," she said to herself. "What are the odds I would open up to that passage? Jon Anderson is a thorn in my flesh."

CHAPTER 10

"Hey, guy!" Chris greeted Jon while opening his front door. Once Jon was inside the living room, Chris shook hands with him the way they had greeted each other as kids. Their secret handshake had not been used in over a year and Jon wondered what Chris was trying to evoke. "Boys for life," Chris laughed, patting Jon on the back and walking toward the couch.

"Where are Sartelli and Jay-dawg?" Jon asked, taking a seat in an oversized recliner.

"Jay's watching the game at Samson's with Matt," Chris said, after taking a sip of Vitamin Water. "Sartelli's hanging out with that girl from his school. Do you want something to drink?"

"Nah, I'm good," Jon replied.

"Feel like placing a bet?" Chris asked. "Jason said they're doing squares at Samson's and we can get in on them."

"I'm good with that," Jon declined.

"I hear ya, bro," Chris said, shaking his head. "I'm too broke to place a bet on the sun rising tomorrow."

"Does Taylor let you keep any of the money your parents leave when they go away?" Jon asked, hoping Chris would bring up the party.

"Ha, are you kidding?" Chris laughed. "I'm pretty sure he blows it up his nose."

Jon shook his head. "Your parents are crazy to leave you with him. Do they have a clue?"

Chris shrugged. "I love the kid; he's hysterical. Actually, Jordan's even funnier, but Taylor's an animal."

Jon took a deep breath, trying to scrounge up enough guts to share his faith with Chris. "Alyssa told me she thinks Lisa is into you," was all Jon could muster.

"Sweet," Chris stated, staring at the TV. "She'd be a good conquest."

"Alyssa told me to tell you that Lisa doesn't like guys who smoke," Jon said, staring hard at Chris.

Chris turned to Jon and smiled. "Then why does Lyss think she's into me? I probably smoked ten cigarettes the night of the party."

"Why are you smoking? Don't you know that's going to weigh you down on the field?" Jon questioned Chris disapprovingly.

Chris shrugged. "I'm not worried about it. It's not like I do it every day."

"Yeah, but what's the point of doing it at all?" Jon asked.

Chris shrugged. "I don't know. It adds to my buzz? I don't have a better reason to give you. It's not something I want to do habitually, but I also don't see anything wrong with it."

"Are you kidding me?" Jon laughed, throwing his arms out. "Why would you risk anything that could hinder your football career? Don't you still want to play pro ball someday?"

"Dude, I appreciate your concern. I would be saying the same thing to you if the situation were reversed," Chris stated calmly. "It's just really not an issue because I don't do it a lot."

"What does Marc say?" Jon asked.

Chris rolled his eyes and turned toward the TV. "He says everything you just said."

"What about drinking?" Jon pressed.

"Guy, chill," Chris laughed. "Did you come over to watch the game or to interrogate me?"

"So, he's against that, too?" Jon assumed.

"Marc doesn't want to follow Taylor's footsteps, so he shies away from what Taylor does," Chris replied. "Marc's only fifteen. Taylor is twenty-one. Marc has plenty of time to corrupt himself. He's just focused on football right now and doesn't want anything weighing him down. He's on Varsity this year, which is kind of huge for a sophomore."

"Of course, he is. His brothers are MLH legacies," Jon stated. "Marc has great skill, but I'm sure Jordan had something to do with his placement on the team."

"Jordan and Marc aren't exactly friends," Chris stated, standing up from the couch. "They almost got in a fight at the party over some girl. I don't think Jordan had anything to do with Marc's placement."

"Why would they let a girl get in between them?" Jon wondered out loud. "They're stuck with each other for life. Girls are a dime a dozen."

"Not this girl," Chris said as he shook his head. "I'm going to heat up some pizza. We have pepperoni and extra cheese. What do you want?"

Jon shrugged. "I'm not that hungry."

"All right, sit tight. Don't start praying for me when I leave the room or anything," Chris said, laughing as he walked past Jon.

Jon sighed.

"Pizza's in the oven," Chris said, returning to the living room a few moments later.

"When do your parents get back?" Jon asked.

"They're flying home now," Chris replied, kicking off his sandals and placing his feet on the coffee table.

"Where's Katie?" Jon asked, referring to Chris's younger sister.

"She stayed at her friend's house this weekend," Chris said carelessly. "Dude, why are you a barrel of questions right now? You get like this when you're trying to avoid something."

"Get like what?" Jon laughed nervously.

Chris threw his arms up in the air, laughed, and shook his head.

Jon bit his lower lip.

"You're obviously worried about me," Chris stated, sounding as calm as usual. "I can read that on your face."

"Well, yeah, I'm worried about you," Jon admitted. "But—"

"—You can say whatever you want to me," Chris interrupted him. "I know you have my best interest in mind. I'm not going to ream you out for seeing things differently than I do. I respect your opinion. I always have. Just say what you need to so we can chill and finish watching the game."

Jon sighed and scratched his ear in procrastination.

"All right, charades. I like this game," Chris said with a smirk. "So, let me start guessing. You're wondering what's going to happen to our fantastic foursome if you keep spending Friday nights at church, while Jay's banging random girls, and Bryan and I are getting lit. Right? Am I right? Cold? Hot? Warm?"

Jon stared at Chris, wondering what his answer would be to his own question.

"I see the wheels turning, Anderson," Chris laughed. "Okay, let's pretend I was pretty hot on that one. My response to that would be there's a lot more to friendship than what we do for fun. You never pressure me into coming to youth group, just like I never pressure you into partying. If you stay completely straightedge until the day you die, you will still be my best friend. You're not my party-buddy, but you've got my back. I can't speak for Jay or Bryan, but you and I are kosher."

Jon nodded and then paused in thought. "I just need some friends who will help keep me in check," he blurted out.

"If you're praying for us to become the type of friends who can keep you in check, then you should probably shift your prayers around a little," Chris said with amusement. "I don't know the future, but I don't see that happening. You should hang out with some kids from your church. There's nothing wrong with having more than one group of friends. We're not going to shun you because you hang out with other people."

"That's cool but, it bothers me to see you guys so attracted to sin," Jon admitted. "You're just robbing yourself of the best by running from God. I'm not going to stop praying for you, because I know God can change anyone's heart."

"See, I'll sit and listen to this stuff because I'm open-minded," Chris said, "but Jay would chew you out. I'm not anti-God by any means, and I totally don't buy into that evolution bull, but I just don't think I'm running from God."

Jon stared at Chris, wishing he had the boldness to point out the ways he had seen Chris run from God. He couldn't muster a single word; his tongue was tied in a knot.

"Honestly, I don't think Jay is anti-God either," Chris added. "When we were little Jay wanted to be a priest. He loved filling his 150-IQ brain with ideas of God."

"Are you kidding me?" Jon laughed after swallowing the large lump in his throat.

"No," Chris shook his head. "When he found out that a bunch of priests had molested kids and that the church covered it up, he went ballistic. He felt like everything he had grown up believing was a lie. He begged his parents to take him out of St. Timothy's, but they wouldn't. He has hated church ever since. I can't blame him. That's twisted."

"So, that's where his anger comes from," Jon said slowly, trying to process Chris's words. "God didn't molest those boys, men did. Only someone with a seared conscience could do something like that. Those priests tore down the name of Christ."

"Look, I'm just telling you this because I don't think you should tell Jay what you just told me," Chris said. "He's got a bad taste in his mouth about religion. If you talk to him, choose your words carefully."

Jon nodded. "Point taken. I bet a lot of people turned away from God because of the priest scandals."

"It made me glad that my family only goes to church on Christmas and Easter," Chris shrugged. "I don't need to hear a pervert tell me I'm a sinner every week."

"Well, my church isn't like that," Jon stated flatly. "It's not based on traditions, rules, or rituals. It's the real deal. Would you ever try it out?"

"Maybe," Chris said and shrugged carelessly. "I'm not against anything you do."

Satisfied with Chris's response, Jon glanced at the football score for the first time. "Tie game!" he shouted, widening his eyes.

"Jordan and Taylor are there," Chris said, rolling his eyes. "My dad left them tickets as a thank you present for watching Katie and me."

"Your dad's in the dark," Jon said, once again wondering if he should tell Chris's parents that Taylor is a disservice to their lives.

"No, he's not," Chris mumbled. "My parents would rather travel freely for their business than worry about leaving us in good care. They're making bank."

Despite Chris's attempt to sound indifferent, Jon picked up on the pain in Chris's tone. Jon battled with the ache of rejection and abandonment daily because of his father. He imagined Chris's pain was much deeper, since *both* of Chris's parents seemed unconcerned with the welfare of their children.

CHAPTER 11

"Oh!" Chantal exclaimed, as her books flew out of her hands and scattered at her feet.

"I am so sorry!" Lisa Ankerman cried, bending down to pick up Chantal's belongings. "I am such a klutz. I didn't even see you. I'm sure this is exactly how you wanted your Monday to start off."

"It's okay," Chantal said, taking her books from Lisa. "You were in my class in fourth grade. Lisa, right?"

Lisa nodded. "Yeah, Lisa who should have her contacts in. I'm sorry."

"It's okay," Chantal giggled. "Aren't you friends with Andy?"

"Yeah, he's pretty much my brother," Lisa said, rolling her olive-green eyes. "He drives me crazy."

Chantal smiled. "I'm pretty sure he thinks the world of you."

Lisa blushed. "I'm guessing you're Chantal?"

"Yeah, Cathy's the twin usually dressed like a guy," Chantal nodded. "You can typically find her in the gym or on the soccer field. She'd probably be on the football field if the school would let her play." Chantal rolled her eyes. "We're so different."

"I have to run to class now, but I'm glad I ran into you," Lisa said. "No, wait. I don't mean that literally!" she laughed, placing her hand on Chantal's arm. "I'm still sorry about that. What I mean is, I'm glad I saw you. Andy has told me a lot about you recently."

"Really?" Chantal asked, sounding surprised to the utmost degree.

"Yeah, really. I have to jet, but you should eat lunch with us today," Lisa stated, flipping her long, dark-chocolate hair over her petite shoulder.

"Thanks, maybe I will," Chantal replied.

"Okay, see ya," Lisa said, rushing past Chantal toward her classroom.

Chantal began walking toward her own classroom while wondering if Andy had put Lisa up to their run-in. Although middle school had only been in session for a month, people had already begun gaining reputations. Lisa was the prettiest girl in their grade and, therefore, acclaimed "popular." Chantal couldn't help but suspect Andy might have had something to do with Lisa's sudden friendliness. Since the first day of school, Lisa had seemed perfectly content sticking with her crew of boys: Andy, Bobby Ryan, and Adam Case. Chantal had never seen Lisa try to befriend a girl in their grade. By the time Chantal entered her English class, she was certain Andy had played a role in Lisa's lunchtime invitation.

Cathy was walking toward her usual lunch table when she felt someone latch onto her arm. She turned to see Lisa Ankerman walking beside her.

"I invited Chantal to eat lunch with me today," Lisa said, letting go of Cathy's arm. "I wouldn't want you to feel left out, so you're welcome to join us. I know you and Chantal are BFFs."

"Since when are you friends with Chantal?" Cathy asked, pausing near her usual lunch table.

"Since I ran her over in the hallway this morning," Lisa said with a laugh as she stopped at Cathy's side.

"I just think it's a little funny that you'd want to befriend her," Cathy stated flatly. "Aren't you best friends with the kid who's been chasing her around this entire school for weeks?"

Lisa laughed. "Yes."

Cathy crossed her arms and stared at Lisa.

"Andy didn't put me up to it. I swear!" Lisa exclaimed and smiled sweetly. "I've just heard a lot about her and thought it would be cool to hang out with her."

"So, you ran her over in the hallway?"

"Okay, I totally didn't mean to bump into her; it just happened somehow. I'm not trying to trick your sister into anything. I'm just being friendly."

"You don't really strike me as the friendly type," Cathy stated, while crossing her arms.

"You don't like the idea of Andy and Chantal, do you?" Lisa asked, cocking her head to the side.

"No, not one bit," Cathy admitted, shaking her head, "but that's not why I'm giving you a hard time."

"Okay," Lisa said, a bit taken aback. "Did I do something to offend you?"

"No," Cathy laughed. "I don't even know you."

"Wow. You and Chantal really *are* different," Lisa stated, looking Cathy up and down. "She's so sweet, and you're just as abrasive as me."

Cathy smiled. "Honestly, I'm just protective of Chantal. She is sweet, and she trusts people way too easily. I wouldn't want her to fall into a trap. I just see you inviting her to eat at Andy's table as a conflict of interest."

"I invited both of you," Lisa responded coldly, "and I would like to sit down before lunch is over. So, I'm going to take a seat at my table, and if you want to join us, feel free."

Cathy watched Lisa walk hastily over to her table and sit down beside Bobby Ryan.

"Hi," Chantal said in her usual cheerful tone as she tapped Cathy on the shoulder.

"Hey," Cathy said, whipping around to face her twin. "So, Lisa Ankerman told me she invited you to eat with her and Andy. She invited me, too, so I wouldn't feel left out."

"Yeah, what do you think about that?" Chantal asked, looking as skeptical as Cathy had initially felt.

"I think Andy's talked you up a lot, and Lisa wants to see if you're really all he makes you out to be," Cathy replied honestly.

"You don't think he put her up to it?" Chantal questioned her.

Cathy shrugged. "He might have, but either way she's interested in figuring you out."

"So, do we go sit over there?" Chantal asked, watching Andy take a seat across from Lisa.

"I'm interested in figuring Lisa out," Cathy said. "You know how I feel about Andy."

"Let's just eat with them," Chantal resounded, glancing again at Andy. "I'm sure Lisa doesn't mean either of us harm. I know you don't like the idea of Andy and me, but you know I'm way more into Jon anyway."

"That's because Jon's a challenge," Cathy said, following Chantal toward Lisa's lunch table.

"No, it's because he's an awesome guy who loves God," Chantal retorted.

"Whatever, Chantal," Cathy snapped, rolling her eyes.

"Well, well, well! To what do I owe this honor?" Andy asked, standing up from his seat as he noticed Chantal coming his way.

"I invited Chantal and Cathy to eat with us," Lisa said. "I didn't think you'd mind."

"Good job, Lis," Andy commended. "Take a seat, girls. There's plenty of room since Troy and Justin are absent."

Chantal took a seat beside Adam Case, one of the smartest kids in her grade. Cathy sulked as she sat down in the only empty chair at the table—next to Andy. Cathy didn't want to despise Andy; she just couldn't help but see him as the phony he was. Andy was exactly who he needed to be at every moment. He was a people-pleasing, quick-witted, eloquent-speaking, charismatic, flirty, manipulative, overconfident charmer. Cathy could not see him as anything else than poison in Chantal's life.

"So, you girls should come to my house Saturday night," Bobby Ryan said, glancing from Chantal to Cathy. "My parents are going out for dinner, so my cousin Pat is watching me. He's a sophomore at MLH. He's cool. He said I could invite some friends over to chill. So, think about it."

"Yes, please come," Lisa said, nodding intently. "I am always the *only* girl, and it gets so old, so fast."

"Why don't you ever bring your cheerleading friends over?" Bobby asked. "I've seen pictures, and those girls are hot."

Lisa laughed. "They don't want to hang out with *you*!"

"Aw, dissed!" Andy exclaimed, clapping his hands together.

"I'm just messing with you, Bobby," Lisa said with a smirk. "They've been busy, but I'll keep throwing the invites their way."

"Score," Bobby said.

"Hey, maybe if Chantal and Cathy come keep you company, Jeff will give you a break," Andy said to Lisa, raising his eyebrows up and down. "Huh?"

Lisa rolled her eyes. "I have another idea of how to take care of that problem."

"The boy's hot for you," Andy said.

"Who's Jeff?" Cathy asked curiously.

"My best friend from Hamilton," Adam spoke up. "Well, actually, he's their best friend, too," he said pointing to Bobby and Andy. "Can't you tell by the way they talk about him?"

"Nah, Jeff's a cool kid," Andy said. "I just like to give Lis a hard time."

"It's not my fault that I don't like boys that smoke," Lisa stated matter-of-factly. "That's why none of you boys should smoke," she added, kicking Andy under the table.

"Oww!" Andy yelped. "What the hell was that for?"

"Nothing," Lisa replied, smiling sweetly. "I just like to give you a hard time."

"Wow, you guys really are like brother and sister," Chantal commented.

"So, think about coming Saturday, seriously," Bobby said, glancing at the twins.

"I have plans with my friend Jessie on Saturday," Cathy said. "I appreciate the invitation though."

"Why don't you bring her?" Bobby asked.

Cathy laughed. "I don't think she'd be too into hanging out with you guys. No offense, she's just more of a girls-night kind of chick."

"Chantal, write your phone number down for me, and I'll give you a call," Lisa said, passing Chantal her assignment notebook. "If you decide that you want to come to Bobby's, then we can go together."

"Okay," Chantal agreed, scribbling her number down.

"You girls made that exchange so easily," Andy snickered. "If I ever said that to her, I would look like the biggest tool."

"That's because girls are way less complicated than guys," Lisa stated smugly.

Andy rolled his eyes. "So, was that lie number fifteen, sixteen, or seventeen of the day?"

"Do you want me to kick you again?" Lisa asked playfully, raising her perfectly shaped eyebrows.

"You two are going to scare away our new friends," Bobby said, shaking his head. "I swear they're not always this lame. Did you guys need to buy lunch? Or are you into that anorexia thing?" he asked, glancing from Cathy to Chantal.

"We have to buy lunch," Chantal replied, slowly standing up from her seat.

"I brought my lunch, but I'll come keep you company in line," Andy offered, jumping up from the table.

"No, it's okay. I've got it covered," Cathy said, pushing Andy back down in his seat. "There's no line, and I'm plenty of company."

"I like her," Lisa said, pointing at Cathy. "She's great."

"Okay, so, we'll be back in a few!" Chantal said nervously and hustled across the cafeteria. Cathy had to run to catch up with Chantal. "That was so awkward!" Chantal exclaimed, once Cathy reached her in line.

"You know me and my honesty," Cathy said. "I despise Andy. I can't hide it!"

"You need to love him," Chantal scolded, picking up her cafeteria tray. "We are supposed love our enemies and bless those who curse us."

"Andy doesn't curse us," Cathy retorted, following Chantal over to the salad bar. "He's just after you for the wrong reasons. I'm telling you, he's poison."

Chantal rolled her eyes. "But he's really nice to me," she whined, turning toward Cathy. "You always see the worst in people. He has a lot of good qualities that everyone can see except you! Can't you see how much the teachers and the students here like him?"

"You know I'm a good judge of character Chantal, and I'm telling you to be careful," Cathy warned her. "I know you don't want to believe any of this, but Andy is bad news."

CHAPTER 12

After school on Monday, Jon laced up his running sneakers and hustled out his front door. He found running to be the best antidote for confusion, and he desperately needed to clear his mind. It was unusually warm for a late September afternoon in Massachusetts. The sky was clear blue, and the air was without the gentle breeze that Jon thoroughly enjoyed while running. Jon realized he would only be able to do a quick run around the lake since the heat index was still in the high eighties.

Jon ran to the end of his street and turned right. Within thirty seconds he was breezing past Chris's street. He reached Montgomery Lake a moment later. As he glanced at the sparkling blue water, Jon thought of his last trip to California. He had wanted to spend the entire summer with his father—in hope of reconciling with him. Over the summer, his father had claimed that he was too tied to his desk to spend a mere weekend with Jon. The only option Jon's father had given him was visiting in September, which meant missing the first week of school. Jon believed his father had made the offer thinking that he would decline. Jon knew his father felt guilty every time he laid eyes on him. Jon believed he was a reminder of everything his father had left behind in Massachusetts. He glimpsed again at the glistening lake, deciding to never abandon anyone who loved him.

The pain of abandonment had been haunting him all day. God had healed his heart tremendously, but visiting his father in California had reopened many old wounds.

"God help me," Jon muttered aloud, hurdling over a large rock that lay at the edge of the lake. *My heart is filled with conflict. I don't want to separate myself from my friends. I don't want to give up on them. I know you can change them. I know they don't have to follow Taylor Dunkin's path. Please intervene. Please send someone into each of their lives who will shine Your light on them. I can't abandon them. They need me. I love them.*

Please put someone in my life that can hold me accountable. I just want a Christian friend who will be able to understand my struggles. If I'm meant to hang out with the boys in youth group please give me the desire to. I have no desire to hang out with them. They don't seem any purer than Chris or Bryan or Jason, besides their verbal claims to be Christians. Please don't ask me to separate myself from my boys. They need me to set a good example. If I stay in Your Word daily and keep up an active prayer life, I know You will keep me strong enough to withstand temptation. I don't want to hurt those guys by abandoning them. Enough people have abandoned Chris already! I can't do it! Please show him how he has been running from You. Please open his eyes so he can see that he is not right with You. He believes in You, but is that enough? There is no way he understands the message of the Cross. If he did, he would not live the way he lives. I know he's not right with You. God help me. I am so burdened and anxious. This can't be right. I'm not supposed to feel this way. Am I not trusting You? Is my heart unaligned with my head? Why do I doubt Your promises? Jon prayed silently, fighting off tears of hopelessness.

Jon picked up his pace as he neared the final bend of the lake. *The Bible tells me that if I leave loved ones for Your sake then You will take care of them and reward me in this life and in eternity. Why can't I see my situation in that light? Why am I having so much trouble figuring out if You are asking me to leave them? Is it because I want to keep my friendships intact so badly? Have my friends become an idol in my heart? Am I putting them before Your will for my life? That's the way I feel, and I hate it! Why does this have to be so hard?* Jon continued, praying in silence.

After completing one lap around the lake, Jon slowed his pace. He spent the remaining time of his run listening for God's response. Jon had always been much better at talking than listening. He was waiting for God to open his mind about something he had not thought of before. The moment of clarity came right as Jon was entering his driveway.

"Oh my gosh!" Jon cried, stopping abruptly in his tracks. His heart seemed to drop to his stomach, and his face lost all color. "Wow," he said, trying to catch his breath. He brought his hands to his face and wiped the sweat from his forehead. He bent over and took a seat on the cement. He looked up at the sky. "I never thought it would happen like this," he said, letting out a heavy breath. He shook his head in disbelief. "Wow, that makes so much sense." He fell over flat on his back and stared blankly at the cloudless sky.

"Hey, are you all right over there?" a loud voice called from across the street.

Immediately, Jon snapped out of his daze and realized how strange he must have looked. "Yeah, I'm great!" Jon yelled to his neighbor as he sat up. "Actually, I'm fantastic!" he added, before running into his house.

CHAPTER 13

"Hi!" Alyssa exclaimed, jumping onto the couch beside Jon and throwing her feet on his lap later that evening.

"Oww!" Jon cried, laughing and pushing Alyssa's feet away. "Your feet reek."

"So, I brought *American Pie 2* and *Wedding Crashers*," Alyssa said tossing the DVDs at Jon.

"Oh, Lyss," Jon groaned. "I don't want to watch either one."

"*Wedding Crashers* is hysterical!" Alyssa cried defensively.

"I believe you, but I'm all set," Jon said, putting the DVDs down on the coffee table. "You know my mom would be appalled if she walked in here and saw us watching either one of those movies."

Alyssa shrugged.

"Sorry," Jon said, smiling slightly.

"Well, I thought something like that might happen, so I also brought this one," Alyssa said, pulling *The Sandlot* out of her pocketbook.

Jon smiled. "Classic," he said, taking the movie from Alyssa.

"Oh, I asked my friend Lisa about your mystery twins," Alyssa said as Jon put the movie in the DVD player.

"Oh yeah?" Jon sang nonchalantly. "Does she know them?" he asked, walking back to the couch.

"She doesn't hang out with either of them, but she is attempting to befriend the girly one," Alyssa replied. "I don't remember who is girly and who is not, but hopefully you know which twin I mean."

"Okay, yeah," Jon nodded, listening intently.

"She was surprised that I was asking about them for you because one of them is going out with her best friend, and the other is really stuck up," Alyssa said, raising one eyebrow. "I told her I had no idea why you asked."

"Wait, what?" Jon asked, shaking his head in confusion. "Which one has a boyfriend?"

"Duh, the nice one," Alyssa said, as if it were common sense.

"I don't know which one the nice one is," Jon replied, sounding somewhat frantic. "I think they're both nice."

"Oh, well, Lisa doesn't," Alyssa stated, shrugging carelessly.

"Well, did she say anything else about the one that has a boyfriend?" Jon asked, lowering his eyebrows.

"What is going on?" Alyssa questioned Jon suspiciously. "You're acting really interested. Yeah, you know what? You're acting like you have a thing for one of them."

Jon cocked his head back and crossed his arms.

"Wow," Alyssa said, widening her hazel eyes. "You actually do. Jon Anderson likes a girl. Jon Anderson likes a girl. You know, I think I'll have to keep saying that for the next hour before I'll believe what I'm hearing."

Jon tossed a pillow at Alyssa's head. Alyssa caught the pillow and reamed it back at Jon. "Oh, I can't wait to see how this turns out. I wonder if you like the one Lisa wants to befriend. I was under the impression that she was trying to befriend the one dating her best friend, but I'm not sure she specified. That would really suck if you finally liked a girl and she was already taken. Good thing you have me to find these things out for you," Alyssa concluded. "I'll find out which one is dating Lisa's friend. What are their names? Chantal and Cathy?"

"Yup," Jon muttered.

"And which one do you like?" Alyssa asked.

Jon shook his head from side to side. "No, I'm not saying a word to anyone. She will be the first to know."

"Not fair!" Alyssa exclaimed, slapping Jon's leg.

"Oh look! The previews are over!" Jon laughed, turning toward the TV. "Haha, I love keeping you in suspense!"

CHAPTER 14

Chantal yawned as she entered her homeroom on Tuesday morning. She had stayed up late to study for a French quiz and was paying the price that morning. It was not even eight in the morning, and Chantal already wanted the day to be over. She set her heavy eyes on her desk in the back of the room and wished it would meet her halfway.

As Chantal neared her desk, she noticed a single red rose lay across it. In an instant the heaviness lifted from her eyelids. Her heart began racing. Her cheeks went flush. Within two seconds she was sitting in her seat and ripping open the card that lay beside the rose.

Join me for lunch today? Chantal read to herself. *You have four periods to think it over. I hope between now and then I can convince you. Hopefully yours, Andy.* Chantal let out an excited laugh and smiled.

"Please don't tell me Andy left you that rose," Cathy said dryly, taking her seat beside Chantal. Chantal brought the scarlet pedals to her nose and breathed in their aroma.

Twenty minutes later Chantal entered her Social Studies class, surprised to see another rose lying across her desk. "Andy," she said affectionately beneath her breath, as she made way to her desk.

Dear Chantal,
You have far too much beauty for just one rose. The red pedals remind me of your long chestnut hair I play with

Chantal read Andy's note, turning a deeper shade of crimson with every word.

"Looks like someone has a secret admirer," Chantal's teacher, Ms. Rice, said quietly. Chantal smiled and began wondering if Andy would have a surprise waiting for her in her next class.

"Chantal and Andy sitting in a tree!" Bobby Ryan sang teasingly as he walked by Chantal's desk.

Chantal blushed and shot Bobby a playful glare.

"Are you going to come over Saturday night?" he asked, sitting down at the desk beside Chantal.

"May-be," Chantal sang, bringing the rose to her lips.

"You should," Bobby nodded. "Lisa would definitely like your company. It's too bad Cathy has plans already; she's a funny girl. It seems like she *hates* Andy."

Chantal rolled her eyes. "Yeah, she does seem to have a special dislike for him. I'm not quite sure why," she stated.

Bobby shrugged. "I think it's funny."

"Are there going to be any other girls at your house besides Lisa?" Chantal asked.

"I told Lisa to invite some of her friends. I hope she does," Bobby replied. "Her best friends are from Montgomery Lake. She met them through cheerleading, way back when. They've been cheering for my football team since I was eight."

"I was kind of wondering if Lisa had any girlfriends," Chantal admitted. "Every time I see her, she is alone or with you guys."

"Yeah, she has girlfriends," Bobby said. "She's just really selective about whom she hangs out with. It seems like she's taken an interest in getting to know you and Cathy though."

Chantal shrugged. "I guess."

"I'm not saying I know what that card on your desk says," Bobby smirked, "but I am saying you should eat lunch with us today."

"I'll think about it," Chantal said, turning to face Ms. Rice at the front of the room.

After Social Studies, Chantal stopped by her locker to pick up her French binder. As she opened the top of her locker, she felt something hit her forehead. "What the heck!" she cried. She picked up the triangular shaped note that had fallen to her feet. She glanced at her watch. She had five minutes until her French quiz began. Throwing the note in her back pocket, Chantal raced off toward the Language Arts Hall.

"So, that Lisa girl from my party messaged me on Instagram last night," Chris said as he and Jon walked toward their second period computer class. "Alyssa must have told her I was @dunkin_85."

"What'd she say?" Jon asked.

"She invited me to Bobby Ryan's house on Saturday night."

"The QB you play football with?"

Chris nodded. "Yeah, I didn't realize she was connected to him. I might go."

"Is Bobby cool with that?" Jon asked. "Isn't he kind of competitive with you on the field?"

"Nah it's fine. Bob's cool," Chris said. "It's just weird that one of my teammates is friends with the girl I'm interested in. I guess Montgomery is a lot smaller than I thought."

"Did Lisa invite Alyssa?" Jon asked as he walked through their classroom's door.

"She said Katherine and Leslie were invited, but she didn't mention Alyssa," Chris replied, following Jon into the classroom.

"I wonder if her best friend is going to be there with his girlfriend," Jon thought aloud.

"Huh?" Chris asked, taking his seat.

"You should go," Jon said, dropping his backpack onto his chair.

"Dude, what?" Chris laughed. "Whose girlfriend? What are you talking about?"

Jon hesitated. "Nothing, guy. I was just thinking out loud," Jon stated in an amused manner.

"Yeah, okay home-slice," Chris laughed and clapped his hands together. "Something's up with you."

"Not this guy," Jon denied, shaking his head and pointing his thumbs at his chest.

"I'll let you know if I end up going," Chris said, turning on his computer. "Lisa's pretty dope. I should probably capitalize on the opportunity."

"I really have to see this girl," Jon commented, taking a seat beside Chris.

"Bobby's cousin Pat is going to be housesitting," Chris said, leaning back in his chair. "He's a cool kid. He's not going to let it get out of control like Taylor does, but I'm sure he won't mind a little tipping of the bottle."

Jon shook his head disapprovingly. "I'll get the scoop from Leslie next period. She always knows what the deal is."

"Right," Chris agreed. "Good thinking. Find out if Katherine's going, too. Jay thought she was pretty cute."

Jon lowered his eyebrows and flipped out his arm in a questioning manner. "Wasn't Jay upstairs that night with a different girl?"

"He sure was," Chris chuckled.

"Katherine Rossi is one girl Jay has no chance with," Jon said with a laugh.

"I've seen Jay win bigger conquests," Chris said.

"Katherine, dude? No. No way," Jon stated, shaking his head. "She's practically mute. I'm shocked she even went to your party."

"Wo-ah bashing Rossi!" Chris exclaimed, widening his blue eyes with amusement. "What'd she do to you?"

"Nothing, man," Jon laughed. "You think I'm bashing her, but I'm actually complimenting her."

"Figures," Chris said. "Still, find out if she's going to Bobby's. I might ask Jay to tag along."

"Thanks for the invite, dude!" Jon cried defensively.

"Would you really want to chill with guys from Sterling?" Chris asked dryly. "I want Lisa. Jay wants Katherine. What the hell would be your motive?"

"I won't see you guys on Friday because of youth group, so I'd like to at least hang out Saturday," Jon replied.

"That's it? No other motive, Jonny-boy?" Chris questioned Jon with a smirk.

"All right, something might be up with me," Jon admitted, letting out a short laugh.

"Talk to Leslie. I'll talk to Lisa. We'll figure it out," Chris resounded. "I'm only thinking of going because of Lisa. I've met some of the Sterling boys, and they're not exactly our type of peeps. Bobby's all right on the field, but I wouldn't make it a point to hang out with him."

"Don't you get it though? Lisa's one of *their* girls. She came to a party at *your* house. Now some of *our* girls are getting invited to *their* places. The girls are starting to overlap," Jon said.

"So," Chris responded flatly. "It doesn't mean we have to. Those kids are pansies."

"I think one of my friends from church is dating one of them," Jon said.

"Then your friend's got bad taste." Chris grinned and widened his blue eyes. "They're all preps over there. Not even like jock-preps— Bobby's an exception. They're like argyle-sweater-wearing preps."

"No, they're not, dude!" Jon exclaimed.

"They might as well be," Chris said flatly, rolling his eyes and shaking his head. "I'm telling you, our competition's weak over there."

CHAPTER 15

Chantal—or can I call you Tal? What would lunch be without dessert? Please accept this box of cookies, along with my lunch invitation. I actually baked these myself—okay, with a little help from Lisa. I look forward to seeing you fourth period.
Enjoy French,
Andy

Butterflies fluttered around Chantal's stomach as her eyes skimmed Andy's thoughtful words. Her smile grew wider with every line of text. Her heartbeat seemed audible by the time she closed his card.

"Please clear off your desks," Chantal's French teacher, Madame Leone, said. "I am going to begin passing out the quiz. You will have half the period to complete it. Please turn it over on your desk when you finish. I will collect them all together."

As Chantal returned Andy's card to its envelope and tucked the box of cookies beneath her chair, the butterflies in her stomach dissipated. *Blonde hair. Brown eyes. A crooked smile. Jon Anderson.* Why had a vision of Jon's attractive face broken through her favorable thoughts of Andy? As she took the quiz from her teacher's hand, Chantal found herself wishing Jon would take a lesson from Andy and pursue her with such candor.

"Vous introduire. D'où vous sont? Quels sont votre aime et déteste? Qui est votre meilleur ami?" Chantal read to herself as her eyes skimmed the first question. She sighed and began writing:

Je m'appelle Chantal Kagelli. J'habite en Montgomery, Massachusetts. J'aime ma famille, mon chien, chanter, Dieu, et les garçons. Je n'aime pas suis confondu des garçons. Je souhaite que je n'étais pas. Ma meilleur amie est ma soeur.

"Hey, Lee! What's kickin'?" Jon asked, jumping on top of Leslie's desk before their English class began.

Leslie giggled. "Jonny, you're wrinkling my homework!" she whined jokingly, pulling a sheet of paper out from beneath him.

"My bad," he apologized. "Are you going to Lisa's friend's party on Saturday? Chris told me about it."

"Oh, she always invites Katherine and me to hang out with those boys," Leslie replied, "but we're not really interested."

"Why not?" Jon asked, envisioning argyle-sweaters.

Leslie shrugged. "I guess we're just not that comfortable around guys. We were even nervous at Chris's party, and we've known Chris since kindergarten!"

"No way. Really?" Jon asked, surprised that someone as outgoing as Leslie would feel that way.

"More so Katherine than me, but, yeah, we're not really used to hanging out with boys outside of school," Leslie admitted. "And the only people we knew at Chris's were Chris and Alyssa. There were a ton of high school kids there. I felt really out of place."

"You met two of my best friends that night," Jon stated, sliding off Leslie's desk. "What'd you think of Bry and Jay?"

"Is that a trick question?" Leslie asked, smiling slightly.

"No, why?" Jon shook his head and eyed her curiously.

"Forget it," Leslie stated quickly and smiled at Jon.

Jon lowered his eyebrows. "Am I missing something?"

"No," Leslie said innocently.

"Okay, so, anyway," Jon said, laughing awkwardly, "you guys aren't going to Bobby Ryan's?"

Leslie shook her head. "No, but I feel bad always saying no to Lisa's invitations. She came with us to Chris's, so I feel like we should go with her to Bobby's. It's just that we don't have any interest in hanging out with a bunch of guys."

"I gotcha. Is Lisa really as pretty as Chris makes her out to be?" Jon asked.

"Yeah, she is," Leslie stated flatly. "Boys from all around Montgomery chase after her. She has the luxury of being able to be picky."

"Do you think she's into Chris?" Jon pressed.

"Who isn't?" Leslie asked matter-of-factly.

"Right," Jon acknowledged. "I was thinking of maybe going with him on Saturday, but I'd be more apt to go if you or Katherine were going to be there."

"Maybe Lisa will invite Alyssa," Leslie said thoughtfully. "They've been in touch since Chris's party. I think Alyssa would go. She's definitely comfortable around guys."

"Yeah she is," Jon sang. "She's over my house just about every day. She's sort of become 'the girl' of my crew."

"Mr. Anderson, please take your seat," their English teacher called out as she entered the classroom.

"Always on my case," Jon said quietly to Leslie, rolling his eyes.

"I'll talk to you later," Leslie whispered, smiling at Jon as he walked across the room.

"So, did you think any more about coming Saturday night?" Lisa asked, pausing at Chantal's locker before third period.

Chantal turned from her locker at the sound of Lisa's voice. "I'm considering it," she replied. "Thanks for helping Andy bake those cookies. Want one?" she offered, pulling the box out of her locker.

"No, thanks," Lisa replied. "He really likes you, Chantal. I've never seen him bake for a girl before. Actually, I'm pretty sure he had never baked in his life. You should have seen him yesterday. He melted the butter in the microwave, instead of just softening it. What a mess! He had to throw the whole first batch away. Actually, he'll probably be embarrassed that I told you, but he gets an A for effort. He wanted everything to be perfect for you."

Chantal's insides melted at the sound of Lisa's words. "Really?" she asked, wearing her appreciation on her face.

Lisa smiled. "Really. Well, I have to jet, but maybe I'll see you at lunch."

"Okay, bye," Chantal said, turning back toward her locker. Suddenly she remembered the note in her back pocket. She reached into her jeans and pulled out the tiny triangle. Glancing at her watch, she decided she had enough time to read it before heading to class. Unfolding the note, Chantal began wondering if it were another part of Andy's plan. She immediately recognized Cathy's handwriting all over the open sheet of paper:

<u>Charm</u> is deceitful and <u>beauty</u> is passing, but a woman who fears the LORD, she shall be praised. – Proverbs 31:30; For such people are not serving our Lord Christ, but their own appetites. By smooth talk and flattery they deceive the minds of naive people. – Romans 16:18; With <u>flattery</u> he will corrupt those who have violated the covenant, but the people who know their God will <u>firmly</u> resist him. – Daniel 11:32; Though his speech is charming, do not believe him, for seven abominations fill his heart. – Proverbs 26:25; Do not be yoked together with <u>unbelievers</u>. For what do righteousness and wickedness have in common? Or what fellowship can light have with darkness? – 2 Cor. 6:14

<u>What are you doing Chantal</u>? You know better than to buy into Andy's charm!!! I love you and that's why I wrote this all out for you. I don't care if you get mad at me. Can't you see how clear <u>God's word</u> is about this type of thing? You said you want to get serious about your walk with God. Are you also considering dating a non-believer? You're being double-minded! Can you not see? Do you not think Jon is worth the wait? I know he's the one you really like. Why would you risk ruining things with him? You have no idea what God has in store for you. He could be about to bring you and Jon together and Satan could be trying to tempt you with Andy. I don't care if Andy surprises you with a <u>dozen</u> long stem roses! Smarten up!
You know I love you,
Cathy

Chantal sighed. She threw Cathy's note loosely into her locker and slammed the door shut.

CHAPTER 16

Andy Rosetti waited anxiously for Chantal to enter his fourth period classroom. He glanced for the third time at the clock that hung above the blackboard. The bell was going to ring in less than a minute. Andy had envisioned Chantal rushing into the classroom, juggling the roses, cookies, and photo album he had given her, and accepting his invitation without hesitation. Perhaps he had scared her off by being so direct? He knew she wasn't absent; both Lisa and Bobby had reported her attendance to Andy. So, where was she? The bell began ringing as a foot, followed by a leg, followed by the rest of Chantal's body entered the classroom. Andy relaxed and leaned back in his chair.

"Just in time, Ms. Kagelli," their teacher, Mr. Sanders said.

"As usual," Chantal replied, quickly taking her seat toward the front of the room. She glanced at Andy and smiled. "Thank you," she mouthed.

Andy smiled in return, anxious for Chantal's feedback. Mr. Sanders usually gave the class a break thirty minutes into the period, but Andy decided he couldn't wait that long. He pulled out a piece of notebook paper and began writing:

Hey, Chantal,

Andy folded the note in a square and wrote Chantal's name on the outside. When Mr. Sanders turned toward the blackboard, Andy passed it to his friend Justin, who passed it to Adam, who passed it to Chantal. The whole transaction took about three minutes. Chantal received the note and tucked it under her book. Because she sat close to Mr. Sanders, Chantal was going to have trouble reading it inconspicuously. Once again Andy found himself stricken with anxiety. He was eager to watch her read the note and even more eager for her response.

When Mr. Sanders began handing out an assignment sheet on metaphors, Andy saw Chantal reach for the note. She slouched in her seat and began unfolding it. Then, she clipped it into her binder and began reading it. *Smart*, Andy thought, *it looks like she is reviewing her English notes.*

From the left side, Andy thought it looked like Chantal was smiling as her eyes skimmed the paper. After a moment she flipped his note over and began writing on a blank sheet of paper. After accepting the metaphor handout from Mr. Sanders, Chantal passed her note to Adam. Andy darted his eyes at Adam to hurry him along. Adam, being as studious as usual, waited for Mr. Sanders to explain their worksheet before passing the note to Justin. Andy's heart beat heavily against his chest as Justin carelessly tossed Chantal's note at him. Andy glanced at Mr. Sanders and let out a sigh of relief; his back was to the class. In one fluid motion Andy tore open Chantal's note.

Andy smiled widely. He glanced at Chantal and gave her a thumbs-up. She blushed slightly and then turned back toward her metaphor worksheet.

CHAPTER 17

"So, Leslie got hung up when I asked her what she thought of Jay and Sartelli," Jon said, leaning toward his knee as he stretched his leg on Chris's front steps after school.

"Oh yeah?" Chris asked, sitting on his lawn and lacing up his running shoes. "I can't quite picture that. Leslie's the most talkative person I've ever met."

"She said she and Kat aren't going to Bobby's," Jon informed him, stretching his other leg. "Maybe you're right dude? Maybe the Sterling guys are geeks? She mentioned a couple of times that she has no interest in them."

"Told ya," Chris laughed. "Bifocal glasses and argyle sweaters. No wonder Lisa came to my party. I'm sure Leslie and Katherine told her what we're like. She fits in perfectly. I bet she and Lyss will stay friends. They both have a strangely attractive wild streak running through them."

"Alyssa?" Jon asked, letting out a short laugh. "What dude?"

"Oh, she's mischievous," Chris mused. "C'mon she fits right in with us. Just wait and see. She'll come out of her shell soon. Any girl that chooses to hang out with me and Jay on a regular basis has to have a love for adventure, sarcasm, and trouble. There's no way around it."

"Maybe," Jon said, standing up straight. "So, Lisa's mischievous?"

"Yeah, but in such a wonderful way," Chris replied. "She threw back just as many beers as Bryan and me, without hesitation. She's not shy at all. She actually made fun of Jay to his face. Now, you know only Matt, Luke, and I are allowed to do that."

"She sounds like quite a catch," Jon said half-heartedly.

"For me dude, not you," Chris stated, touching his toes. "You're probably the only guy I know who wouldn't be into her."

"Hey, good thing we don't have the same taste," Jon said. "You know how competitive we are in baseball; can you imagine what we'd be like with girls?"

Chris laughed and jumped to his feet. "Race ya to the lake!" he shouted while breezing past Jon.

"Chantal, will you please open your door?" Cathy pleaded, turning Chantal's locked doorknob back and forth.

"Go away!" Chantal retorted. "I'm not mad at you. I just don't feel like talking to you right now."

"If you weren't mad, then you'd want to talk," Cathy replied. "I know you're mad."

"Leave me alone!" Chantal demanded. "You are so annoying."

Cathy sighed, rolled her eyes, and walked away from Chantal's door.

***

"Thanks for the invitation, but I doubt my parents will let me go," Alyssa said to Lisa on the phone Tuesday night.

"Really?" Lisa asked in surprise. "But they let you go to Chris's?"

"Well, yeah, they know Chris."

"And they let you go?!"

"I know, shocking right?" Alyssa giggled. "No, my parents know I hang out with Chris, Jon, Jason, and Bryan all the time. The only girls I hang out with are Leslie and Katherine. The rest of the girls in my grade are pretty lame."

"I hear ya on that," Lisa stated. "It'll be awesome when we're all together at MLH. It's cool getting to know some of you guys from other schools. By the time we get to high school maybe we'll already have a clique to be in."

"Jon and the guys have been dreaming about high school since third grade," Alyssa said dryly. "Poor Jason. He's tucked away at an all-boys school. That kid likes girls more than any guy I know."

"Probably because he's surrounded by sausage, all day every day!" Lisa exclaimed.

"Probably," Alyssa agreed. "Chris told me that Jay thought Katherine was cute. I couldn't even tell her. I think she'd throw up!"

"She would!" Lisa cried. "Katherine was horrified by him. Not only because he went upstairs with that girl, but also because of his language and cruel jokes. I thought he was hilarious, but she's ultrashy."

"I know!" Alyssa shrieked. "I was shocked that she even agreed to come. She is not even friends with Chris. Leslie must have twisted her arm."

"I had more fun watching her facial expressions that night," Lisa giggled. "I love Katherine to pieces. She's just so innocent that it's funny."

"She's like the girl version of my friend Jon," Alyssa stated. "He's the one who asked me about those twins from your school. It made no sense to me because he has zero percent interest in girls, usually."

"Yeah, I want to meet that kid," Lisa said. "Chris talks about him all the time. He sounds like a good guy."

"He's my best friend," Alyssa stated. "Jon's awesome. He's just really into his church, and it's so funny because his best friends are totally opposite. In some ways Jon actually makes Katherine look wild."

"That's hysterical. I don't think anyone could make my little Kit-Kat look wild," Lisa stated with amusement. "You said he's friends with the Kagelli twins from church, right?"

"Yeah, I guess they're in his youth group," Alyssa replied. "I wish I knew more about them, but Jon's really discrete. I'm not sure why he wanted me to ask you about them."

"I'm actually really starting to like Chantal," Lisa said. "I had to help Andy bake cookies for her yesterday. He is *so* in love. It's wicked funny because usually Andy's the one being chased after. To see him fall head-over-heels for someone has been quite entertaining. She's been cautious with him, which makes it that much better. I'm not sure if she's an expert at mind games, or if she's just hard to win over. We invited her to Bobby's on Saturday, and even after Andy showered her with presents, she didn't give him a straight answer."

"So, wait. They're not boyfriend and girlfriend yet?" Alyssa asked.

"I don't know what they are," Lisa replied dryly. "They've made it clear to our grade that there is something between them, but I don't know what they're calling it."

"Is she really pretty?" Alyssa asked.

"Well, I think the twin-factor makes her attractive," Lisa said thoughtfully. "For some reason guys seems to dig that type of thing. But yeah, she's pretty. She has long reddish-brown hair and warm green eyes. She's thin and feminine and meek. I can see why Andy's into her."

"So, she's the girly one, the nice one, and the one your best friend is with?" Alyssa asked.

"Right," Lisa replied. "I'm actually starting to like Cathy, too. She's funny. I mean not in, like, a Jay or Chris way but in a weird way."

"How so?" Alyssa asked curiously.

"I guess I was wrong to say she's mean," Lisa continued. "I think she's just more blunt than the average girl. I sometimes cast off a snobby attitude purposely, but it doesn't faze Cathy. She could care less if I like her. Personally, I like that. I don't care much for people pleasers—aside from Andy and Leslie."

"Do a lot of guys from your school like Cathy?" Alyssa asked.

"I think the guys are intimidated by her," Lisa said honestly. "I mean, she's made it clear that she doesn't like Andy. Andy's the best catch in my grade. So, if she doesn't like him, then the guys can't expect her to like them either. They all look up to Andy."

"Andy sounds kind of like Chris," Alyssa said. "Everyone likes to follow his lead."

"In that sense they're alike, but personality wise they're very different," Lisa commented. "Chris is like what-you-see-is-what-you-get. Andy is like three-thousand shades of grey. He's complicated."

"What do you mean?" Alyssa asked with a short laugh.

"Like I said, he's a people pleaser. So, basically, he is whatever he needs to be at a given moment. He can be the responsible Class President and then the kid drinking vodka out of a water bottle seconds later."

"Is he bi-polar?" Alyssa asked.

"No!" Lisa cried, trying to contain her laughter. "He's just really good at manipulating people. Everyone sees him how they want to. All of our friends' parents love him; the teachers love him; our class idolizes him. He's really charismatic. He knows how to make people feel good about themselves. Bobby, Adam, Jeff, and I are probably the only ones that get to see all his different shades."

"So, is he trying to manipulate Chantal?" Alyssa asked, finding it odd that Lisa would want to be friends with someone so shady.

"Oh, I don't think so," Lisa replied quickly. "He really likes her a lot. He's definitely trying to treat her right. I don't think he has dishonest intentions."

"Oh, that's good," Alyssa commented.

"Andy's not a deceptive person; he's just good at charming a crowd," Lisa explained. "He's an awesome kid. I guess he just knows how to balance a diverse lifestyle."

"Then he's not really like Chris at all," Alyssa concluded. "Chris is not much of a people-pleaser. He kind of sounds like Cathy."

"Yeah, I guess he kind of is," Lisa agreed. "Cathy just seems to have a strong sense of who she is and what she believes in. I wouldn't want to argue with her. Chantal is much more easygoing and gentle. Cathy can see through Andy, and that's why she doesn't like him."

"I can see why Jon is intrigued by the twins. I'm kind of intrigued myself," Alyssa admitted. "Maybe if I go to Bobby's, I'll get to meet them."

"Cathy won't be there," Lisa said, "but I bet Andy will woo Chantal into coming."

"I wish a guy would chase after me like that," Alyssa said. "The guys I know don't put effort into girls. The girls just fall at their feet. You should give Chris a good challenge. He's used to girls making a big deal out of him."

"Trust me," Lisa said, "I know how to play my cards with guys like him."

"Good," Alyssa stated flatly. "I'll ask my parents and let you know if I can go with you. We could go together, right?"

"Yeah sure," Lisa said. "My brother J.C. could give us a ride."

"All right, awesome," Alyssa said. "I'll call you tomorrow or something."

"Great! Talk to you then," Lisa sang happily.

"Bye!" Alyssa cried, hanging up her bedroom phone. She paused for a moment of thought before dialing Jon's number.

CHAPTER 18

Jon was lying on his bed and reading his Bible, when his cell phone began ringing. Putting his book aside, Jon flipped open his phone. "What's up, Lyss?"

"Hey, are you sitting down?" Alyssa asked.

"Lying down," Jon replied.

"Oh, even better. I just got off the phone with Lisa and found out some more information about your twins," Alyssa informed him.

"Oh really?" Jon asked, sitting up straight and closing his Bible. "Please tell me that you know who's single!"

"I kind of think they both might be," Alyssa said hesitantly. "It was weird. Lisa started telling me about how her best friend Andy is trying to win over Chantal. He's gone to great lengths to get her to have lunch with him. She said he is trying to convince her to go to Bobby's party on Saturday. She said that Chantal is either really good at mind games or really hard to get. So, that made me think they're not boyfriend and girlfriend yet."

"I see," Jon said slowly.

"I asked Lisa, and she said it's obvious something is between them," Alyssa continued, "but she didn't know what to call it."

"Okay," Jon said, "so it's Chantal who might be dating Lisa's friend? Is she the one Lisa thought was nice?"

"Yeah, well I guess she is starting to like both of them," Alyssa replied. "She said Cathy is kind of blunt, like Chris, and Chantal is really sweet."

"Cathy? Blunt?"

"Yeah. Lisa said Cathy made it clear she doesn't like Andy, and that she tells it like it is," Alyssa stated matter-of-factly.

"Cathy is *so* quiet at church," Jon stressed. "She pretty much hides behind Chantal. She won't even pray out loud. I actually asked her once why she was so quiet."

"Did she say she wasn't?"

"Actually, I think she did," Jon replied thoughtfully. "Or Chantal might have said that. I don't remember. But that's weird. Okay, so they both might be single?"

"Jon," Alyssa spoke seriously, "I really hope you don't like Chantal. I would hate to see you get hurt. You don't understand what you would be up against. Lisa's best friend, Andy, he's like the leader of the pack. Lisa said he's Class President. She said he's been pursuing Chantal for a while—with presents! It sounds like he's got a lot to offer, and I'm not saying you don't, but I just think you'd have some steep competition."

"Thanks for your concern, Lyss. What did Lisa say about Cathy?"

"Nothing really," Alyssa replied. "She just said Cathy's funny and outspoken, oh, and that the guys are intimidated by her. She said Cathy knows who she is, and that she doesn't try to please people."

"Did Lisa invite you to Bobby's party?"

"Yeah, but I don't think I'll be able to go," Alyssa answered. "His parents aren't going to be home and you know how strict my dad is."

"Isn't Bobby's cousin friends with your brother?"

"Pat Ryan? I think so."

"Maybe if your dad finds out that they're friends, he'll let you go?" Jon reasoned.

"That's a thought," Alyssa said. "My brother's been kind of distant from his friends lately. I'm not sure what's up with him. He even broke up with the mayor's daughter."

"Really?" Jon asked. "Wow, they were together for a while."

"Yeah, for like three years," Alyssa agreed. "I'll find out if he's friends with Pat though. Maybe it could work to my advantage."

"Cool."

"You know, I can't tell from anything you've said which twin you're interested in."

"Are you're surprised?"

"You are so discrete!"

"Thanks for all the valuable information, Lyss," Jon said. "You're the best."

"Lisa said I could go with her to Bobby's, and she also said that she invited Chantal. So, hypothetically, I could be hanging out with one of your twins on Saturday."

"Hmmm… Montgomery becomes smaller by the day," Jon said with a laugh.

"If that happens, do you want me to ask her about you?"

"I'm pretty sure that Lisa would not be a fan of that," Jon replied. "She obviously wants Chantal to be with her best friend."

"Ooh, this could get ugly!" Alyssa exclaimed. "I mean, if it is *Chantal* you're into, and you and Andy start competing for her, that could cause a problem for Leslie, Katherine, and me. We're all friends with Lisa."

"You have runaway-mind," Jon said light heartedly.

"This is getting kind of exciting!" Alyssa cried with a spark of mischief in her tone.

"All right, goodnight, Lyss," Jon said, rolling his eyes.

"See ya tomorrow!" Alyssa giggled.

Jon shut his phone and fell back onto his bed. "Okay," he said out loud, taking a deep breath. "God, I know your voice. I know I do. Nothing is impossible with You. Somehow this is all meant to be. Somehow, You're going to work this out. Am I supposed to go with Chris to Bobby's? Why is my life entangling with these people from a bunch of different directions? Could some of them be the Christian friends I have been praying for? Chris said they were on the innocent side. Help me not to get carried away in wonder. I know I need to live in the present because that is where You meet me. I lift Cathy and Chantal up to You now, and I pray that You bless them tonight, and keep them from dating anyone who is not from You. Please show me what to do. How am I supposed to act on this?"

CHAPTER 19

Thursday afternoon, Chantal lay on her bed filing her nails. She was trying to decide if she wanted to call Andy or wait for him to call her.

"Oh, you're home?" Cathy asked, halting in front of Chantal's bedroom doorway. "I thought you were at Lisa's."

"Huh?"

"Lisa told me that Andy was going to invite you over her house."

Chantal lowered her eyebrows in confusion and peered at her twin.

Cathy shrugged. "I must have gotten the days confused. Anyway, Jon and I are going for a run. He's jogging here right now."

After the comprehension of Cathy's words, Chantal felt as though her insides were filling up with fluid and drowning her heart. The fluid seemed to travel to her eyes, and she fought to keep it contained.

"Well, I'll see you later," Cathy said, waving goodbye and continuing down the hallway.

Chantal remained completely still on her bed for the next five minutes. She was afraid that if she moved, the tears welling up inside of her would cause a deluge in her bedroom. The ringing of her nearby telephone interrupted her disheartening vision of Jon and Cathy walking down the aisle together. "Hello?" she called halfheartedly into the phone.

"Is Chantal there?" a boy's voice responded.

Chantal's heart began to pound. "This is Chantal."

"Guess who this is."

"Hmmm… without looking at my caller ID?"

"Caller IDs ruin all the fun!"

"Well, this is obviously someone who likes playing games," Chantal commented, feeling her mood begin to lighten.

"Ha, that's one way to put it," the boy laughed.

"I give up," Chantal said.

"That easily? Boo, you're no fun. Are you sure this isn't Cathy?"

Chantal laughed. "Okay, now I know it's you—Andy!"

"What's up? You sound kind of down, my friend," Andy said.

"It's nothing," Chantal replied quickly. "Cathy's just annoying me."

"Is she still hating on the idea of you and me?"

"Actually, she seems much less opposed to it today," Chantal said. "Figures," she added.

"Maybe my charm has won me some points."

"Yeah, your charm or someone else's charm."

"O-kay. Anyway, I'm heading over to Lisa's in a few. She's having people over to watch the game. Do you want to go with me?"

"Sure!" Chantal exclaimed, without a second thought.

"Just like that?" Andy asked.

"Yup! Just like that."

"All right, nice. I can be at your house in twenty minutes. Sound good?"

"Perfect!" Chantal replied as a smile began spreading widely across her face.

Twenty minutes later the Kagelli's doorbell rang. Hustling down to the first floor, Chantal passed Cathy on the stairs. "You didn't leave yet?" Chantal asked.

"No, where are you running off to?" Cathy asked curiously.

"To Lisa's with Andy," Chantal replied as she whipped open the front door. Expecting to see Andy, Chantal felt her heart leap in her chest when her green eyes grazed Jon's attractive face. "Oh! Hi!" she exclaimed.

Jon lowered his eyebrows and peered at Chantal. "Chantal?" he asked quietly.

"Yeah, come in," Chantal replied, opening the door widely. "Cathy's inside." Chantal noticed Jon's perplexed expression as he stepped into the Kagelli's foyer.

"Hi, Jon!" Cathy cried, jumping off the last step to the foyer's tile floor.

"Hey," Jon said. "Ready to give me a good challenge?"

Chantal was shutting the door behind Jon when she noticed Andy jogging up her driveway. As she glanced at Cathy and Jon, her stomach dropped at the sight of them standing so closely together. "Have a great run, guys," she said, struggling to muster up any words at all. "Andy's here."

"Where are you headed?" Jon asked, glancing out the open door at Andy.

"Oh, to my friend Lisa's house," Chantal replied.

"Have fun," Jon said, smiling awkwardly. As Chantal stepped out the door, she couldn't help but wonder why Jon had seemed so surprised to see her.

CHAPTER 20

"I'm surprised you agreed to come with me," Andy said, as he and Chantal climbed Lisa's front steps. "I'm glad, of course, but surprised. It must be my lucky day!"

Chantal smiled. "I guess you caught me at the right time!"

Andy opened Lisa's front door without knocking and led Chantal up a set of stairs. "Hey, guys," he said, greeting Lisa, Bobby, and Adam as he entered the living room.

"Hey, dude. Hey, Chantal," Bobby called, nodding in Chantal's direction.

"Hi!" Chantal said brightly as she took a seat beside Andy on the couch.

"My dad ordered us pizza," Lisa announced. "The game starts at 5:05."

"Is Jeff coming?" Andy asked, directing the question toward Lisa.

"He has soccer practice," Adam said.

"But you know he'll be over after," Bobby laughed, winking at Lisa. Lisa flipped her middle finger in Bobby's face and frowned.

"I'm kind of curious to meet this kid," Chantal said quietly to Andy.

"You'll like Jeff," Andy stated assuredly. "Well, not as much as Lisa does, but enough."

"Andy Rosetti!" Lisa screeched, tossing a pillow at his head.

Andy caught the pillow and chuckled. "Someday he'll break through her mile-high wall. He's the most persistent guy I know."

Lisa rolled her eyes. "Chantal, are you coming to Bobby's on Saturday?"

"I haven't really decided yet," Chantal replied. "I have youth group tomorrow night, but I'm not sure what my deal is for Saturday."

"You love youth group!" Andy said, letting out a short laugh.

Chantal nodded. "Yup, I do."

"What is youth group, Chantal?" Bobby asked.

"Every Friday night there's something fun to do at my church," Chantal said. "There are kids there from Hamilton, the Lake, Sterling, and a few other towns."

"What do you guys do?" Bobby asked.

"My pastor talks to us about seeing God at work in our lives, which is really fascinating, and then we do something social," Chantal replied.

"Can anyone go?" Andy asked.

"Anyone under eighteen," Chantal said.

"You should check that out," Bobby said, nodding toward Andy.

Andy smiled at Chantal. "I was thinking the same thing," he said.

"You would come with me?" Chantal asked, smiling back at Andy.

Andy laughed. "You'd let me?"

"Come!" Chantal exclaimed, while patting Andy's leg. "And if you hate it, then you never have to come back."

"If it means I get to hang out with you two days in a row, then I'm willing to give it a try," Andy said, patting Chantal's hand.

"You guys are cute," Bobby said sarcastically. "Maybe Jeff should get some tips from Andy on how to get Lisa to hang out with him."

"Don't give him any pointers, Andy," Lisa said. "He'll waste his effort. I'm interested in someone else."

"I know that," Andy replied.

"You know *who*?" Bobby questioned Andy.

"No, he doesn't," Lisa stated. "You'll all find out if anything comes of it."

"Ever since you went to that Lake party, it seems like Sterling isn't cool enough for you," Bobby commented in his usual facetious manner.

Lisa laughed. "Well, after you've partied with MLH's football team your bar gets set a little higher."

"Were you with MLH kids or MLMS kids?" Chantal asked.

"Both," Lisa replied. "My friends, Leslie and Katherine, go to MLMS, and the party was at their friend Chris's house. He has cousins that go to MLH."

"Chris Dunkin?" Chantal asked. "I heard about that party."

"You did?" Andy asked, looking at Chantal strangely. "How?"

"Oh, from Jon Anderson?" Lisa questioned Chantal.

"Yeah! How'd you know that?" Chantal asked. "Do you know Jon?"

"No, I don't know Jon," Lisa answered. "My friend Alyssa is good friends with him, and she told me that he goes to church. I put two and two together."

Chantal stared blankly at Lisa for a few seconds, wishing Jon's name had not come up.

"I know Anderson from town sports," Bobby said. "Actually, I know Dunkin even better. He's a pretty sick football player."

"Chris is Jon's best friend," Chantal said. "I've never met him, but he sounds like a cool kid."

"Small world," Andy said.

"Seriously!" Chantal laughed.

"Isn't Cathy friends with Jon, too?" Lisa questioned Chantal, raising a single eyebrow.

Chantal's heart sank. "Yeah," she replied. "They're actually hanging out right now."

Lisa's face lit up. "Really?" she asked, sounding excited by the news.

"Good luck to him," Bobby stated dryly. "No offense Chantal, but your sister is kind of scary."

"I'm actually starting to like her," Lisa commented.

Andy laughed. "You just like how much crap she gives me!"

"No, that's just what I like best about her!" Lisa teased him.

"Cathy's really cool," Chantal said, setting aside her jealousy. "She just has really strong opinions and a very direct way of making them known."

"That's weird, though, because she comes off as shy at first," Bobby said. "Then she comes out with smart comments that no one can argue with."

"She's slowly coming out of her shell at school," Chantal said. "She's completely out of it on the soccer field, but she's really shy at church, for some reason."

"Why would she be shy at church?" Andy asked. "Isn't that where she should feel most comfortable?"

Chantal shrugged. "That's where I feel most comfortable, but Cathy and I aren't too much alike."

Bobby laughed. "That's for sure!"

At the sound of the doorbell, Lisa cried, "Pizza's here!" She ran out of the living room and down the stairs to the front door. Thirty seconds later she returned without pizza, but with a stunningly attractive blonde-haired, blue-eyed boy wearing a soccer uniform.

"JB!" Andy exclaimed, rising off the couch to slap hands with the boy.

"What's up?" the boy asked, greeting everyone in the room.

"Jeff, this is Chantal. Chantal, this is Jeff," Andy said.

"Hey, Chantal. I've heard a lot of good things about you from this guy," Jeff stated, nodding toward Andy.

Chantal smiled, wondering why Lisa was not interested in the gorgeous, athletically built boy in front of her. "I've heard about you, too."

Jeff laughed. "Only terrible things, I'm sure," he said, taking a seat between Adam and Lisa on the couch opposite Andy and Chantal. "It's all most likely true."

"Did your practice get out early?" Lisa asked Jeff in a softer tone than her usual.

"No, I just ran straight here instead of going home first," Jeff replied.

Chantal was waiting for a teasing remark to come out of Andy's or Bobby's mouth, but the boys spared Jeff and began discussing the upcoming baseball game.

CHAPTER 21

"But Mom, he's only coming because he likes Chantal!" Cathy cried out in protest on the way to youth group Friday evening.

"God can use anything and anyone to attract someone to Himself," Mrs. Kagelli stated.

"Tell her she's being narrow-minded, Mom!" Chantal exclaimed. "Tell her she's supposed to love Andy!"

"Cathy, even if you think Andy's motives are impure, it is impossible for you to know his heart," Mrs. Kagelli said calmly. "Only God knows where Andy's at, and you should be glad that he is going to church with you tonight."

"Andy is so full of himself that there is no room for God to even enter his heart!" Cathy exclaimed dramatically.

"Can't you see how much she hates him, Mom?! Do you see what I have to listen to every day?" Chantal cried out in frustration.

"Cathy, I'm not sure where all this hatred is coming from—"

"—Jealousy!" Chantal interrupted her mother.

"What?!" Cathy shrieked. "I would never be jealous of that lying scumbag!"

"No, you're jealous of the attention he pays me," Chantal accused. "You hate seeing me happy!"

"I am not jealous of you!" Cathy yelled. "I wouldn't want his cookies or his flowers. I wouldn't want to touch Andy with a ten-foot pole!"

"Both of you need to lower your voices and change the subject—immediately!" Mrs. Kagelli rebuked them. "We'll be picking Andy up in one minute, and there is no reason why he should sense any animosity in this vehicle."

Chantal fought off the urge to pull Cathy's ponytail, while Cathy rolled her eyes and pouted against the passenger side window.

Jon had just left Alyssa's house to go to youth group when Alyssa's phone began ringing. Hoping it was someone inviting her out, Alyssa answered.

"Hey, girl, it's Lis!"

"Oh hi," Alyssa replied. "What's up?"

"I wanted to call you earlier, but I was tied up with cheer practice," Lisa said. "The weirdest thing happened yesterday."

"What?"

"Chantal Kagelli came over my house with Andy, and somehow your school came up. She mentioned that she'd heard of Chris, and that led to mention of Jon. Then she told me that Jon was hanging out with Cathy! So, Cathy must be the one he's into," Lisa explained.

"Really?" Alyssa asked. "I was totally putting my money on Chantal."

"But this is so much better! Now we don't have to worry about Andy and Jon competing with each other," Lisa reasoned.

"That's a good point!" Alyssa said. "That's actually a huge relief because I'd hate to see Jon get hurt."

"And I'd hate to see Andy get hurt," Lisa said.

"So, are Andy and Chantal an official couple yet?" Alyssa asked.

"Who knows," Lisa replied. "I don't even know if she's coming to Bobby's tomorrow. She surely doesn't act like seeing Andy is a priority to her."

"Oh, about Bobby's… I can't go," Alyssa said sadly. "My parents said I could only go if my brother went, too."

"Your brother won't go?"

"No, he said he's all set with seeing Pat Ryan. John's pulled away from that entire crew."

"Oh, boo," Lisa whined. "Well, hopefully Chris will have another party soon. It's cool that you're allowed to go over his house."

"Is Chris going to Bobby's?" Alyssa asked.

"He told me he'd let me know tomorrow. I think he has something against Sterling guys."

"Chris? He doesn't usually have anything against anyone."

"Well, he said he didn't want to overstep his bounds, but I told him Bobby wouldn't mind if he came. I think Chris is going to talk to Bobby at football practice tomorrow."

"If he shows up, then you'll know he likes you a lot!"

"Hopefully," Lisa sighed. "Hey, have you ever gone with Jon to youth group?"

"No, I'm Methodist," Alyssa replied.

"Oh, 'cause Andy is on his way there now with Chantal."

"Andy's religious?"

Lisa laughed. "Not at all."

"Does he want to be?"

"I doubt it."

"Is he trying to be who he thinks Chantal wants him to be?"

"No, I think he just wants a better understanding of what makes her tick."

"Oh, well, then that's cool," Alyssa said. "So, that means Jon and Andy are going to meet tonight."

"I feel better about that now, knowing Jon is into Cathy."

"Me too!"

"The way that you've described Jon made me a bit surprised to hear that he was hanging out with Cathy," Lisa admitted. "I mean, he sounds so nice, and Cathy's pretty harsh."

"I guess we'll understand when we see them together," Alyssa said.

"I think it's so funny how much all of our paths are crossing," Lisa commented. "Six degrees of separation has become one degree of separation!"

"Seriously!"

"Oh! Chris is beeping in!" Lisa exclaimed.

"Answer it!"

"Okay! I'll talk to you later, girl."

"Have fun talking to Chris. Bye!"

"Later!"

CHAPTER 22

Jon was making small talk with one of the boys in youth group when Cathy came rushing through the door. Her face was as red as her hair, and her feet were barely touching the ground. Jon waved to her. "What, are you practicing your speed for our next race, or something?" he teased her, as she rushed to his side.

Cathy laughed. "I think it's your speed that needs the practice!"

"Oh! Disssss!" Jon exclaimed.

Chantal walked through the door a second later with the boy Jon had caught a glimpse of at the Kagelli's. Chantal glanced around the room and locked eyes with Jon. She smiled slightly. Jon noticed a hint of sadness in her eyes. He wondered about the cause, and if his eyes mirrored her look.

"I'm sitting with you tonight," Cathy said as she took a seat diagonally behind Jon.

"Don't you and Chantal usually roll in together?" Jon asked, turning around to face Cathy.

"Yeah, but Mr. Perfect took my place tonight," Cathy replied sarcastically.

"Is he from your school?" Jon asked.

"Oh, he's basically President of my school," Cathy responded.

Jon nodded. "Well, don't you think Chantal deserves a boyfriend like that? I can see her as Sterling's First Lady."

"He doesn't deserve her," Cathy stated flatly.

Jon watched as Chantal introduced the boy to Jessie and the other kids sitting nearby. The boy seemed very friendly and extremely happy to be by Chantal's side.

***

Saturday morning Jon awoke to the ringing of his cell phone. "Sup," he said groggily.

"Hey, guy. We're trying to get a game together at Sartelli's by noon. You in?" Chris asked, sounding way too awake for ten o'clock.

"Ya, ya," Jon replied. "Just give me another hour of sleep and I should be good. Why are you so awake?"

"I'm on my way home from football practice," Chris said. "I'm good to go."

"All right, man. I'll see ya at Sartelli's later," Jon said, whipping his blankets over his head to block out the sunlight that was pouring in through his window.

"Cool. Oh, if you want to come to Bobby Ryan's tonight, it's cool," Chris added. "I talked to Bobby at practice. He seemed surprised that Lisa invited me."

"You're going to give Sterling guys a chance?" Jon asked.

"For Lisa," Chris replied. "Plus, I know Bobby's all right, so his friends can't be too bad."

"You're really into this girl," Jon said.

"I'm into seeing where it goes," Chris corrected.

"Well, dude, I'm all set with going," Jon stated downheartedly. "I met one of Bobby's friends last night, and I've had my fair share."

"At church?" Chris asked.

"Yeah, he came with a friend of mine," Jon replied.

"Bad news?" Chris asked.

"For me," Jon stated flatly.

"Hey, guy, never let the fear of striking out keep you from playing the game," Chris said. "I'll see you at Bry-guy's."

"All right, man. Peace."

"Later."

CHAPTER 23

Chantal walked into her kitchen Saturday evening and glanced at the clock. Andy and his mom would be picking her up in less than ten minutes. She glanced down at her outfit: a deep purple sweater dress, black leggings, and furry black boots.

"Chantal you look so pretty!" Jessie exclaimed from the breakfast nook, where she was sitting with Cathy.

"Thanks," Chantal said, smiling brightly. "I'm going over Andy's friend's house."

"Fun!" Jessie cried, smiling back at Chantal. "Andy's really cute, Chantal."

"He is," Chantal agreed. "You two were invited tonight, you know. You could still come," she said, glancing from Jessie to Cathy.

"Really? Whose—"

"—No, we're staying here!" Cathy stated abruptly, interrupting Jessie.

Jessie glanced at Cathy quickly, and then turned back toward Chantal.

"Okay…well, have a good night," Chantal said with a slight shrug in Jessie's direction, before exiting the kitchen.

Chantal and Andy arrived at Bobby's house fifteen minutes later. Andy took Chantal's hand as they climbed the front steps. "I'm really glad you're here," he said as Chantal's stomach fluttered. "My friends like you a lot," he added.

"I like them, too," Chantal said, smiling widely.

Within seconds of Andy ringing the doorbell, Bobby whipped open the door. "Hey, guys," he greeted them. "Head downstairs. Lisa's down there making the punch. We just ordered a bunch of food from Ding's."

"Nice," Andy said. "You hungry?" he asked, turning toward Chantal.

Chantal shrugged. "I already ate dinner, but I'm always hungry!"

Andy laughed and led Chantal through Bobby's kitchen to the basement stairs.

"Hey!" Lisa greeted them with glistening eyes and a bright smile as they entered the basement.

"Hi," Chantal said, taking in her surroundings. She was standing in a billiards room with a maroon felted pool table in the center. There was a granite topped mahogany bar with five mahogany barstools in front of her. A room with two tan leather couches and a flat screen TV was adjacent to the billiards room. Looking around, Chantal concluded that Bobby's basement resembled a classy hotel lounge. "This is nice!" she exclaimed.

"There's a game room off that hallway," Lisa said, pointing behind the bar area. "Ms. Packman is a fun time."

"Bobby's dad owns a vending company," Andy said, "so, he's always getting new games. We get to try them out for free. It's pretty sweet."

"That's awesome," Chantal said. "Show me the games!"

Ms. Packman, an air hockey table, a racecar game, and an old-fashioned jukebox outlined the game room, which had a central dance floor. "Do Bobby's parents have a lot of parties?" Chantal asked as she glanced around the room.

"I think Bobby gets the most use out of all this, but his parents have thrown a few good ones," Andy replied. "Christmas Eve is happening over here."

"How many people are coming tonight?" Chantal asked as she paused to read the jukebox's song list.

"I never know," Andy said. "You can play any song you want."

"Um, *Livin' on a Prayer?* Classic!" Chantal cried, pressing the code into the jukebox.

"You dig Classic Rock?" Andy asked.

Chantal laughed. "My dad is a big fan, so I'm very familiar with it."

"Nice," Andy said, putting his arm around Chantal's waist. "The more I learn about you, the more I like you!"

Chantal smiled and walked with Andy back into the billiards room. Adam and Jeff had arrived with a few other boys Chantal recognized from school: Troy Rogers, Justin McKnight, and Mike Sanders.

"Andy, we started a list," Lisa said, holding up a piece of paper. "Do you and Chantal want to play?"

"Do you play pool?" Andy asked Chantal.

"I have, but I'm not great at it," Chantal replied.

"Sign us up," Andy said to Lisa.

"Oh, the punch is ready," Lisa chimed. "Bobby's still upstairs, waiting for the food to arrive."

"Do you want some punch? Or there's soda and water in the fridge behind the bar," Andy offered Chantal.

"What kind of punch is it?" Chantal asked, glancing at the large bowl of multicolored liquid.

"Lisa calls it Jungle Punch," Andy replied. "The rainbow sherbet makes it all the funky different colors."

"Oh, that's fun!" Chantal cried. "I'll try it."

"Are you sure?" Andy asked hesitantly.

"Why do you say it like that? Is it gross or something?" Chantal questioned Andy.

"No, it's good," he laughed. "Sometimes it's stronger than other times, so drink with caution."

"O-kay," Chantal said slowly, not quite sure what Andy meant.

Andy poured two glasses of punch and then led Chantal into the TV room. "Bobby's parents said we could order any movie we want, so since I know you have great taste in media, why don't you pick something out?" Andy suggested as he sat down on one of the couches.

"Really?" Chantal asked, picking the remote up off the table. "I might need your input. There's way more guys here than girls, and I don't think I have very masculine taste in movies."

Andy laughed. "Pick whatever you want. Comedy is always a good choice."

"Hey, guys, I'm going to pull out the table and put the food on it," Bobby said as he walked into the room with a couple of boxes and bags.

"Ooh, what'd you order?" Chantal asked, widening her eyes.

"Well, we got some calzones, buffalo wings, pizza, chicken dippers, mozzarella sticks, and curly-fries," Bobby replied, pulling the coffee table across the room with the food on top of it.

"Sweet!" Chantal exclaimed.

Andy laughed. "You really do love food, huh?"

"I'm passionate about food!" Chantal said. "By-the-way, this punch is really good."

"Yeah, Lisa does a good job with it," Andy agreed.

"It's so sweet though. I'm glad the food's here to balance it out," Chantal added.

"Eat up," Bobby said, opening the last tray of food. "If we run out, we'll just order more."

"What do you think about *Meet the Parents*?" Chantal said, scanning the long list of comedies on demand.

"Put it on for now," Andy replied. "We can always change it later."

"All right," Chantal said, selecting the movie and then resting the remote on the couch. "Bobby's a good host, huh?" she remarked quietly.

"Oh, yeah," Andy said, nodding. "He's used to it. We do this a few times a month."

"I wish Cathy and Jessie had come," Chantal stated. "They would have liked this."

"I met Jessie last night, right? Your pastor's daughter?" Andy asked.

Chantal nodded.

"She seems really nice. Actually, all the kids there were nice," Andy said.

"Except…"

"Cathy."

"Right."

"Right."

"She's been acting like she hates me," Chantal said. "I don't know what her problem is."

"You guys have always been best friends, right?" Andy asked.

"Yeah," Chantal said.

"Well, maybe it's like what your pastor was talking about last night," Andy said thoughtfully. "Maybe God wants you and Cathy to shine for Him in the world, instead of just sticking to each other."

"So, you *were* listening last night?" Chantal giggled.

"Of course, I was," Andy said. "It kept my interest."

"You'd come again?" Chantal wondered.

"If you invite me, and if you can guarantee that Cathy won't plot my death, then yeah," Andy replied.

"Cool," Chantal said. "Maybe you're right. Maybe God does want Cathy and me to broaden our social circles."

"You're a good influence on people, Chantal," Andy complimented. "I can't see why He wouldn't want that."

"Thanks," Chantal said, blushing slightly. "Will you split a piece of calzone with me?"

"Ham and cheese?"

"Deal!"

"Andy! Chantal!" Jeff called loudly from the billiards room. "You guys are up next."

"Mmmm this calzone is awesome," Chantal said, after taking her first bite. "I might want my other half back!"

"You probably should eat my half to balance out that cup of punch you just downed," Andy said.

"Let's get more punch!" Chantal cried brightly, grabbing ahold of Andy's arm and pulling him into the billiards room.

"Chantal, you do realize that—"

"—Lisa! More of your punch!" Chantal called out, cutting Andy's words off.

Lisa laughed. "Drink up, girl."

"Andy, come talk to me," Jeff said, motioning Andy toward the game room.

"I'll be right back," Andy said to Chantal, leaving her by the bar with Lisa.

"Okay," Chantal said carelessly.

"Jeff's not happy," Lisa whispered to Chantal.

"Why? What's wrong?" Chantal asked, leaning in closely to Lisa.

"Bobby told him that I invited Chris Dunkin here," Lisa replied. "Jeff's pissed."

"Is Chris coming here?" Chantal asked.

Lisa nodded. "Pray there isn't a fight!"

Chantal widened her eyes. "Did you and Jeff used to go out?"

"We hooked up once—that's it—over the summer," Lisa whispered. "It was nothing more than a kiss—not to mention we were both a little drunk—but he's been obsessed with me ever since!"

"You guys were drunk?" Chantal asked.

"Yes! Which is exactly why it shouldn't even count," Lisa reasoned.

"Are you ready to show Adam and Troy how to shoot pool?" Andy asked, placing his hands on Chantal's shoulders as he appeared behind her.

"Sure," Chantal said, picking her and Andy's cups up off the bar.

"Go easy on this," Andy said, taking his cup from Chantal. "Too much punch could easily cost us the game. Adam and Troy are drinking water."

Chantal lowered her eyebrows and eyed Andy thoughtfully. He almost made it sound like the punch was alcoholic. After what Lisa had shared, Chantal realized alcohol was not taboo to the group. Chantal looked down at her cup. The juice tasted like nothing more than Sprite, sherbet, and pineapple juice. Deciding that Andy would know better than to offer her alcohol—and that asking him would probably offend him—Chantal picked up a pool stick and left all thoughts of the punch's consistency behind her.

CHAPTER 24

"Mom, I'm going out with Marc," Chris called loudly up the stairs from his living room. "I'll probably crash at his place."

"Tell Marc I said hi," Mrs. Dunkin replied from her bedroom.

Chris walked out his front door and sat down on the concrete steps. He pulled a little nip of rum out of his cargo pocket, unscrewed the cap, and shot it back in one fluid motion. His eyes were watering and his mouth was burning when Jordan and Marc pulled up in Jordan's Jeep. Chris jumped off his steps and hustled to the driveway. He grabbed hold of the Wrangler's bars and hopped in the backseat.

"Hey, Little D," Jordan greeted Chris.

"Thanks for the ride," Chris said. "Glad the top's off."

"Who's the girl?" Jordan asked, while backing out of Chris's driveway.

"This girl Lisa from Sterling," Chris replied. "She was at our last party."

"I remember her," Marc said. "Dude, if the Sterling guys give you a hard time, then you can just chill with my friends. Pat invited a good crew tonight."

"Yeah, I'm not worried about it," Chris said. "I thought Jay was going to head over with Matt, but he decided to go to Newport with his parents."

"To their summer house?" Marc asked.

"Look at the weather. It sure feels like summer," Chris replied.

"Did Pat invite Michelle over?" Jordan asked.

Marc glanced at Jordan in an unamused manner.

"What?" Jordan laughed. "Did he?"

"Stay away from her," Marc stated—for what seemed to be the hundredth time.

"Hate me for saying this, but I'm going to nail her by graduation," Jordan said.

Chris watched with slight amusement as Marc's face turned bright red. "I know Michelle is hot and all, but what else is it that has you so caught up?" Chris questioned Jordan. "I mean you're the captain of the football team. You could get anyone."

"He doesn't even know her," Marc said. "She's nothing to him but a conquest."

"C'mon dude," Jordan laughed. "A virgin, as hot as Michelle, anyone would want! Marc's just bitter because he didn't score when he had the chance."

Marc let out a heavy sigh and shook his head from side to side.

"Or, he might actually be in love with her," Jordan added, smirking at his younger brother.

"Stop!" Marc yelled.

Jordan, knowing he had gotten on Marc's last nerve, changed the subject. "We're almost at your friend's place. Just call me if you guys need a safe ride home."

"Ha, yeah right," Chris said with a quick laugh.

"How was football this morning?" Marc asked, turning around to face Chris.

"It blew getting up that early, but Coach made me the captain; so, it was worth it," Chris replied.

"Aw, Little D's following right in our footsteps," Jordan sang.

"That's good, Chris," Marc said. "Stay focused."

"I sure have enough people telling me that lately," Chris commented dryly.

"That's because we all know you have enough talent to go far with football," Marc said. "We all knew Taylor did, too, and we know he messed it up. No one wants to see you follow his lead."

"Always so serious, Marky," Jordan laughed. "Drink a few beers at Ryan's and lighten up a little."

Marc rolled his eyes. Chris laughed. Even though Marc and Jordan rarely got along, Chris enjoyed their dynamic. Jordan, who seemed to float through life without a care in the world, could lighten anyone's mood with his humor and playful nature. Marc, although sometimes a bit too serious, could always be counted on for encouragement and wise advice. As opposite as the brothers were, they balanced each other out well. Chris felt more at home with them than he did with his immediate family.

Jordan dropped Marc and Chris off at Bobby's two minutes later. Pat welcomed them inside and told them where to find the food and drinks. Chris recognized all of the sophomores gathered in the living room: Matt Davids, Laurelle Mahoney, Ricky Samson, Bob O'Donnell, Katie McKnight, and Michelle Taylor.

"Chris, Bobby and his friends are downstairs," Pat said. "You can chill up here with us or go down with them."

"I told Lisa that I'd meet her here," Chris said. "She's down there, right?"

"Lisa!" Pat sang and clapped his hands together. "Nice, buddy. Yeah, she's down there."

Chris left the comfort of the MLH sophomores and ventured downstairs to the unfamiliar zone of Sterling seventh graders. His vision of argyle sweaters and bifocal glasses was dashed when his eyes met with a bunch of kids that looked like they modeled for American Eagle.

"Chris!" Lisa exclaimed from behind the bar. She ran around the bar and pool table to meet him by the stairs.

"Hey!" Chris greeted her, widening his aquatic-blue eyes as he took in her beauty. "You look good," he whispered in her ear as he hugged her tightly.

"I know," she said and winked at him, as she pulled free from his embrace. "Come, let me make you a drink. I'm on bartender duty tonight," Lisa laughed, leading Chris toward the bar.

"Straight to the bar, huh?" Chris laughed.

"Introductions can come later," Lisa said with a smile. "We have Jungle Punch—kind of sweet—or there's soda, water, and a little bit of cherry vodka."

"What's the deal with the punch?" Chris asked, looking at the red, orange, and green liquid that filled up one third of the punch bowl in front of him.

"It's just rainbow sherbet, Sprite, vodka, and pineapple juice," Lisa said, stirring the punch.

"Sounds very sweet," Chris said. "I think I'll just grab a beer from upstairs. Unless you want to take a shot of cherry vodka with me first."

"Ye-ah," Lisa sang. "Let me just find some shot glasses."

"Red cups are fine," Chris said, taking two cups from the stack on the bar. "Just fill them to the first line, bartender."

"To be chased with coke?" Lisa asked, grabbing a can of soda out of the fridge.

"Why are you so comfortable behind a bar?" Chris asked curiously.

"Well," Lisa began, pouring some vodka into a cup, "I hang out with kids who started drinking in fifth grade, and my dad has a full-sized bar in our family room. He's quite the connoisseur of exotic liquors."

"Oh really," Chris said. "What does your dad do for a living?"

"He's a lawyer," Lisa replied. "A lawyer with great taste in fine wine and cognac."

"Your friends started drinking in fifth grade?" Chris asked, glancing at the kids in the room.

"Well, not everyone," Lisa said. "A lot of these kids don't drink at all. You'd never get Bobby to take a sip of this punch."

"I figured that much," Chris stated.

"See that kid over there on the couch with that girl," Lisa said, pointing to the TV room.

"Yeah."

"That's my best friend, Andy," Lisa said. "He's my biggest partner in crime."

"Oh, I see," Chris said, turning back toward the bar. "Cheers to the merger of MLMS and Sterling," Chris said, holding his cup up in the air.

"Cheers," Lisa sang, tapping Chris's cup before throwing her cup back.

"Ugh, chaser please," Chris said, reaching for the can of coke as soon as his cup touched the bar.

"Me first!" Lisa whined, pushing Chris's hand away and grabbing the soda.

Chris puckered his face as he waited for Lisa to finish. He grabbed the can from her hand before it touched the bar.

"For someone who has been drinking since fifth grade, you certainly rushed for that chaser," Chris teased her.

"Oh, I haven't been drinking since then," Lisa said, shaking her head. "I waited until this summer. That's when I realized I enjoy the excitement of sneaking around."

"Really?" Chris asked. "I hate having to sneak around. I just like what alcohol does to my mood."

"Your mood?" Lisa asked. "You're the most fun kid around this town."

"Well, thanks," Chris said.

"Do you want me to introduce you to everyone now? Or would you rather get a beer upstairs first?" Lisa asked.

"Doesn't matter," Chris replied with ease.

"Come meet Andy," Lisa said, stepping out from behind the bar and grabbing Chris's hand. She led Chris around the pool table and into the TV room. Chris noticed that Andy and the pretty, auburn-haired girl were sitting very closely. He assumed she was his girlfriend.

"Hey, Lis," Andy said, sitting up straight. "Who's this guy?" he asked in a friendly tone.

"This is Chris," Lisa replied.

"Hey, man, I'm Andy," Andy said, standing up to shake Chris's hand. "Thanks for coming by."

"And this is Chantal," Lisa added, gesturing toward the girl on the couch.

Chantal glanced up at Chris and waved. Then she rested her head on Andy's shoulder. Lisa looked from Chantal to Andy and lowered her eyebrows in concern.

"It's nice to meet you, Chris," Chantal mumbled quietly. "Sorry, I'm just really sleepy for some reason."

"It's cool," Chris said, realizing that Chantal was on the verge of passing out.

"Lisa, do you think Chantal could sleep over your house tonight?" Andy asked.

"Ye-ah," Lisa said hesitantly. "Is she okay?"

Andy widened his eyes and shrugged.

"I'm good," Chantal murmured. "I just have to use the bathroom," she said, standing up slowly.

"Do you want me to take you?" Andy asked. "The bathroom's right off the game room."

"I'm good," Chantal assured him, while staggering out of the room.

"Lisa, do you have Cathy's cell phone number?" Andy asked, once Chantal was out of the room.

"No," Lisa replied.

"If we could get ahold of her and ask her to call her mom, pretending she is Chantal, then she could ask to sleep over your house," Andy said.

"Is Chantal a twin?" Chris asked.

Lisa nodded.

"I can probably get Cathy's number for you," Chris said.

"How?" Andy asked.

"My friend Jon is friends with her," Chris replied.

"Oh, yeah!" Lisa cried. "Aren't they going out?"

Chris looked at Lisa strangely. "Who the heck have you been talking to?"

"Alyssa," Lisa replied.

"Ha, Jon's not with Cathy," Chris stated, shaking his head. "He's not into her *that* way. He also wouldn't tell Alyssa if he was."

"He was with her last night at youth group the whole time," Andy said. "I thought they were together, too."

"Jon just has a knack for being friends with girls," Chris said. "They gravitate toward him. I'm his best friend, and he won't even talk to me about the girl he likes."

"Then how do you know it's not Cathy?" Lisa asked.

"Because he talks to me about her like he does about every other girl we're friends with," Chris shrugged. "They're running buddies and church friends. No more. No less."

"I don't feel so well," Chantal said, as she returned from the bathroom.

"Let's go get some fresh air," Andy suggested, grabbing onto Chantal. "If you could work on getting that number, Chris, that would be great. Call her if you get it."

"All right," Lisa agreed.

As Andy and Chantal disappeared through the slider, Chris turned to Lisa and asked, "Does that girl usually drink?"

"I don't think so," Lisa replied.

"What did she drink tonight?" he asked in a tone that displayed his concern.

"The punch," Lisa said. "Three or four cups."

Chris widened his eyes. "Was she on a mission to get lit?" he asked.

Lisa shrugged. "I don't think so. I mean, she knew she was going home at ten."

"Did anyone tell her that there was vodka in the punch?" Chris asked.

"I assume Andy did," Lisa replied carelessly. "Let's try to get Cathy's number."

"Why don't we just ask Chantal?" Chris asked.

"She's so out of it," Lisa said, "and I don't think she'd agree to deceiving her parents. She won't realize that it's the smart thing to do."

"I thought she was passed out when we came in here," Chris said.

"Her phone!" Lisa suddenly exclaimed, picking Chantal's pocketbook up off the couch. "Cathy's number must be in it."

"You're just going to go through her bag?" Chris questioned Lisa.

"Girls can do that," Lisa replied, unzipping Chantal's bag. "No phone," she said after a few seconds. "She might not even have a cell phone."

"Sounds like you guys need a better plan," Chris said.

"Chantal is Andy's responsibility right now," Lisa stated. "If he let her get that drunk, then he'll figure something out. I don't want to kill your time here by trying to clean up Andy's blunder."

"Let's check on her in a bit," Chris said.

"Okay," Lisa agreed. "It's nice of you to be so concerned."

Chris shrugged. "It sucks to get that sick."

Lisa nodded in agreement. "Let's go upstairs. Afterwards, I'll introduce you to everyone else."

"Sounds like a plan," Chris said and followed Lisa into the billiards room.

CHAPTER 25

Out in the backyard, Andy held Chantal's hair off of her face while she kneeled over and vomited. "You can't go home like this," Andy said. "Your parents will never let you hang out with me again."

"Please… call… my mom," Chantal said, between heaves.

"Why don't you try to eat something first?" Andy pressed. "You've got to sober up."

"Sober up?!" Chantal cried, widening her eyes and looking up at Andy. "What are you talking about?"

"You're sick because you're drunk," Andy stated flatly. "You drank four cups of punch in an hour."

"There was alcohol in the punch?!" Chantal cried angrily. She sat down on the ground and brought her knees to her head.

"Plenty of it," Andy replied, kneeling down beside Chantal.

"This is the worst feeling ever," Chantal moaned, returning to all fours.

"Do you want me to get you some water? Or some food?" Andy offered.

"No, just call my mom and ask her to come get me," Chantal said, wiping sweat from her forehead.

"Chantal, do you really want your mom to see you like this?" Andy asked. "I think you should sleep at Lisa's."

"I want to go home!" Chantal exclaimed. "Why won't you help me?"

Andy sighed. "I'll call your house right now," he said. "Do you want me to say you're sick?"

"Say I'm sick to my stomach," Chantal stated impatiently.

"Chantal, I'm really sorry," Andy said. "I thought you knew there was alcohol in the punch."

"Why... would... you ever... think... I'd drink?" Chantal gagged. "I didn't even think... you... did."

"I don't drink that often!" Andy cried. "I would have drunk water all night if you hadn't gone after the punch."

"Just... call my mom!" Chantal cried.

Andy sighed and retrieved his cell phone from his pocket. "Chantal, I feel bad. I got you into this mess, so your parents should not have to come out. Why don't I ask my mom to come pick us up?"

"Whatever," Chantal said, putting her head in her hands. "Just get me home."

"Hey, Little D!" Marc greeted Chris as he and Lisa entered the family room. "How's the party below?"

Chris glanced around the family room. ESPN was on the TV, there was an open thirty-rack of beer on the table, and everyone at the table was holding cards. "I think I like this scene better," Chris replied. "What are you guys playing?"

"Just a little card game Matty D came up with," Marc said. "We call it Dingle Hopper—don't ask."

"Do you want to stay up here?" Lisa asked Chris quietly.

"I just want to stay with you," Chris responded immediately.

Lisa smiled.

"I'd invite you guys to join the game, if I didn't think Marky-Marc would whip my you-know-what for giving you booze," Pat said and laughed.

Chris looked at Marc and took note of the soda can in front of him. "Can't we just play with soda?" Chris asked.

"Sure," Pat replied with ease. "We'll deal you in next round. Give us, like, five minutes, okay?"

"Are you cool with that?" Chris questioned Lisa.

Lisa nodded. "I like learning new games."

"Okay, we'll be back," Chris said. "Do you want to introduce me to your friends now?" he asked, turning toward Lisa.

"Sure," she replied and led him back downstairs.

"Okay, bartender," Chris said once they reached the billiards room. "How quickly can you fill two cans of soda with punch?"

"Ooh! You're bad!" Lisa laughed and playfully nudged Chris.

Chris grabbed hold of Lisa's arm and spun her into him. "And you're hot," he said.

Lisa locked her olive-green eyes on Chris's baby blues. They were inches away from being nose to nose. Right when Chris began leaning in to kiss Lisa, Lisa spun around and tugged on Chris's arm. "Let's get punch!" she exclaimed.

Chris laughed and, in one fluid motion, picked Lisa up off the ground and spun her around.

"Ah!" Lisa giggled, as Chris carried her like a bride to the bar.

"You're so tiny," Chris commented, still holding Lisa in his arms. "I see why they're able to toss you so high during my football games."

"You've seen me cheer?" Lisa asked.

Chris laughed. "Duh. You cheer for my team."

"Well, I'm glad you noticed," Lisa said, resting her hand on Chris's shoulder.

Again Chris leaned in to kiss Lisa. This time, she hesitated only slightly before meeting him halfway.

CHAPTER 26

"Andy!" Jeff called, hustling into the backyard.

Andy glanced at Jeff and then turned immediately back to Chantal.

"Oh @$%#!" Jeff said, once he saw Chantal. "What's wrong with her?" he questioned Andy, as Chantal keeled over with dry heaves.

"Jungle Punch," Andy said flatly. "Evidently it was not non-alcoholic."

"Is it ever not?" Jeff asked.

Andy rolled his eyes. "She didn't know that, and I didn't tell her."

Jeff peered at Andy in disbelief. "You finally got the church-girl to go out with you, and you gave her spiked punch?!" he cried. "What kind of drugs have you been smoking, guy?"

"I know. I effed up," Andy said. "I'm just hoping she stops dry heaving before my mom gets here."

"More pizza just came," Jeff said. "Why don't you see if she can hold some down? I'll go get her a piece."

"Okay," Andy said. "Grab a bottle of water for her, too."

"You got it," Jeff said as he turned and sprinted toward the house.

"Are you feeling any better?" Andy asked, kneeling down beside Chantal.

"Stay away from me," Chantal demanded.

"Chantal, I am so sorry," Andy said. "Please forgive me. I'm an idiot! I thought you knew there was alcohol in the punch. I thought you were just trying to have fun."

"This is not fun, Andy!" Chantal cried.

"Jeff's getting you food and water," Andy said. "Is there anything else I can get you?"

"Get me to my bed," Chantal replied, glaring at Andy.

"I'm working on that," Andy said.

"I can't believe Cathy was right," Chantal said, sitting up and resting her head against the backyard's fence. "She said hanging out with you would get me in trouble."

"You don't have to get in trouble," Andy said. "You sound a lot better now. Why don't you ask your mom if you can sleep over Lisa's tonight? Trust me, her dad won't notice that you're drunk. My mom could bring you guys to her house."

"My parents trust me," Chantal replied. "I'm not going to lie to them! They're not going to get mad at me because I accidentally drank spiked punch. They'll either suggest that I stop hanging out with your friends, or they'll tell me to avoid punch at parties. For all they know, one of the high school kids could have spiked the punch. I'm not going to tell on Lisa."

"You're so good Chantal," Andy stated. "No wonder your parents trust you. You're open and honest, and you hold to your integrity. Those are some of the things I like most about you."

"Then why are you trying to get me to lie to my parents?" Chantal asked.

"I wasn't asking you to lie," Andy said. "I was just offering you another place to stay in case you didn't feel comfortable going home like this."

"Whatever," Chantal sighed.

"Well, here comes Jeff with the pizza," Andy said, watching Jeff close the basement's slider. "You think you'll be able to hold it down?"

"I can't tell if I'm nauseated or hungry," Chantal replied. "I'll try to eat and see what happens."

"Here, Chantal," Jeff said as he knelt down beside her. "Try drinking some water first. If you can hold that down, then give the pizza a shot."

Chantal nodded and took the bottle of water from Jeff. She took a few small sips of water and then gave the bottle back to him.

"It's okay to take it slowly," Jeff comforted. "Andy's mom won't be here for at least fifteen more minutes."

"Thanks," Chantal said appreciatively.

"Do you feel like you're going to throw up again?" Jeff asked.

"Not yet," Chantal replied.

"Do you want to take a bite of this pizza?" Jeff asked.

"Give me a minute," Chantal said softly.

As Jeff nodded, Chantal noticed the compassion in his eyes.

"Chantal, if you're not throwing up anymore, then maybe you shouldn't risk putting food in your stomach," Andy reasoned. "You seem like you've sobered up."

"You do seem sober," Jeff commented. "Twenty minutes ago, you looked like an ambulance ride waiting to happen."

"Does everyone inside know that I'm sick?" Chantal questioned Jeff.

"I don't think so," Jeff said. "I didn't know until I came outside."

"Why did you come out here?" Andy asked. "You seemed kind of frantic."

"Oh," Jeff sighed. "Lisa was making out with her friend behind the bar. They're probably still at it. The sight drove me crazy. I don't know what her problem is. I know she likes me."

"Lisa was making out with Chris?" Andy asked, widening his eyes. "Wow. She's on top of her game. I'm sorry to hear that, dude. I know you're really into her."

"Maybe she does like you, and that's why she's pushing you away," Chantal suggested. "She might be afraid of her feelings."

"She's not pushing *Chris* away," Jeff said.

"Well, maybe she doesn't like him enough to be scared of getting hurt," Chantal replied. "You can be attracted to someone and still like someone else."

"True," Jeff agreed. "Yeah, Chantal, I'd say you're sober enough now. I'll let Andy be a gentleman and take it from here." He handed Andy the pizza and water, and then went back into the house.

"I ruined my chance with you, didn't I?" Andy asked, sitting down beside Chantal.

"I can't think about that right now," Chantal stated, resting her head in her hands.

"Okay," Andy said. "Do you want some more water?"

Chantal lifted her head and took the water bottle from Andy. "I'm exhausted," she said. "I hope I don't pass out in your mother's car."

"Drink your water," Andy said. "I'll worry about that."

CHAPTER 27

Chantal cried herself to sleep Saturday night. When she awoke Sunday morning, her head felt like it was being drilled, and her stomach felt like it had been turned inside out.

Mrs. Kagelli stayed home from church to comfort Chantal. "Drink more water," she said, as she sat on Chantal's bed and handed her a bottle of water. "You're dehydrated."

"Mom, I'm so angry!" Chantal cried. "I wish I never hung out with Andy. I'm so disappointed in him."

"Apologizing to your father and me the way he did last night was very commendable," Mrs. Kagelli said. "I don't think he meant to get you drunk. Andy and his friends have grown up without relationships with God, so they're going to be more attracted to sin than you are. That is why it's important for you to be a light in their lives but not a follower of their paths. The man is the natural leader in a relationship. Until Andy finds God, he is going to be walking in darkness. You shouldn't want someone leading you who is in darkness."

"I know, Mom," Chantal whined. "I'm just so sad about Jon liking Cathy. When Jon asked Cathy to go running the other day, it made me so upset that I agreed to hang out with Andy just so I'd feel better about myself. Andy made me feel so cherished and special. He had me on a pedestal. Then when he asked to come to youth group, I thought maybe it was good to get closer with him. When Cathy hung out with Jon all night at youth group, it bothered me enough to make me accept Andy's invitation to Bobby's."

"Chantal, things are not always what they seem," Mrs. Kagelli said. "True, Cathy has been talking to *and about* Jon a lot lately, but she is not one to have a crush. I also don't think using Andy's attention as a Band-aid was a very good idea."

"Oh Mom, it's so much worse!" Chantal cried, covering her eyes with her hands. "Jon's best friend was at the party last night. He saw me with Andy. He saw me drunk. I vaguely remember meeting him; I was so out of it. I have prayed for him before—that he wouldn't get caught up in alcohol. Ha! And look, there I was, puking in the backyard."

"Does he know you didn't mean to drink?" Mrs. Kagelli asked.

Chantal shrugged and rested her head against her headboard.

"You know Chantal, if I run into Mr. or Mrs. Ryan, I'm going to tell them about what happened to you. They need to know that underage drinking took place in their home," Mrs. Kagelli stated.

"Andy and his friends will probably hate me if you say something, but I don't really care," Chantal said. "I should have known better than to give into Andy's charm. He really seemed like a good person."

"I know you're mad at him right now, but try not to pass judgment on him," Mrs. Kagelli exhorted her. "Andy may be the great kid you thought he was. At your age kids are faced with many different temptations. It is good that he got exposed to the gospel and to a purer way of life. You never know what impact you may have had on him."

"See, I thought I could be a good influence on him, and I also enjoyed his attention," Chantal admitted. "So, hanging out with him seemed like a win-win situation. I never thought I'd end up making a fool out of myself. I can't wait until my grade hears about it."

"You told me that Andy has a lot of pull in your class, right?" Mrs. Kagelli asked.

Chantal nodded.

"If he is trying to get back on your good graces, then I don't think he's going to let rumors fly," Mrs. Kagelli reasoned. "Also, I doubt Bobby wants it getting around that kids were drinking at his house."

"Andy knows he lost his chance with me," Chantal said.

"Maybe that will make him reevaluate his actions," Mrs. Kagelli shrugged. "I have some housework to get done, but I want you to cheer up. God has a way of working everything together for good."

"Thanks, Mom," Chantal said, smiling slightly. "Don't wake me up until dinner. I feel terrible."

CHAPTER 28

Monday morning, Andy waited at Chantal's locker and nervously tapped his fingers on his science book. The dark circles around his eyes made it obvious that he had hardly slept over the weekend. Thoughts of Chantal and distress over his own idiotic behavior had continuously plagued his mind. The infamous, "if only I had done this," and "if only I had not done that," phrases had been dominating his thoughts since Saturday evening. Andy had more regrets than he could count on his fingers and toes. He was desperate for a second chance with Chantal. His heart ached as he hoped for an opportunity to reconcile with her.

First came Cathy, hustling into the locker hall. She was dressed in her maroon and black soccer uniform, and her auburn hair was pulled back into a ponytail. Then came Chantal, trailing about ten feet behind Cathy. She was wearing a floral sundress with white flip-flops. Her hair was flowing freely past her shoulders. Andy marveled at her beauty and wondered why she had even given him a chance.

When Cathy spotted Andy standing at Chantal's locker, she widened her cat-like green eyes and whipped around to face Chantal. Chantal stopped short and glanced at Andy. Immediately, a look of paranoia washed over her face, and she turned around to stalk out of the locker hall. Andy's heart sank. He had feared that very reaction. He opened his science book and pulled an envelope out of it. As he slipped the card into Chantal's locker, he prayed to God that she would read it.

"Did you see her?" Lisa asked, appearing behind Andy. Andy turned to Lisa and nodded. "Did she talk to you?" Lisa asked.

"She ran the other way once she saw me," Andy replied.

Lisa laughed. "I'd love to see you dig yourself out of this hole."

"It's not funny, Lis," Andy said, shaking his head. "She's really hurt."

"Hurt, embarrassed, ashamed, disappointed—I can continue with the list if you'd like," Lisa stated.

"She doesn't deserve to feel any of that," Andy said. "I should have realized she was too innocent to expect alcohol in the punch. When she asked me what was in it, I was too afraid to mention the vodka. I didn't want her to think we were a bad group of kids."

"We're not," Lisa stated defensively.

"Oh, really?" Andy asked. "Do you really believe that?"

"Andy, we're all great students, good friends, talented athletes, and class leaders," Lisa said, lowering her eyebrows. "Those are good things."

"Then why the heck were we drinking at Bobby's?" Andy questioned Lisa. "When did just hanging out with each other stop being fun enough?"

Lisa shrugged. "I don't know. You and Jeff were the ones who thought drinking was a good idea."

"Well, it was a stupid idea," Andy retorted. "I knew how to have a hell of a lot of fun before I ever took a sip of alcohol."

"Chantal's changed you," Lisa stated flatly.

"No, she hasn't," Andy replied. "She just reminded me of who I really am."

Lisa crossed her arms and frowned.

"Come-on, I'll walk you to Homeroom," Andy said, setting his hand on Lisa's shoulder.

"Fine," Lisa said, stepping away from Chantal's locker. "Chris invited me to his house Friday night."

"Oh yeah?" Andy asked, walking toward Lisa's homeroom.

"He said I could invite all of you guys, too," she said. "His cousin is throwing another party."

"He likes you, huh?"

"So, he says."

"And you're into him?"

"He's a good kisser."

"Ha, what about Jeff?"

"What ABOUT Jeff?"

"Isn't he a good kisser, too?"

Lisa pushed Andy in the shoulder. "Get off the Jeff train for one minute, will you? Chris is really cool."

"All right," Andy surrendered. "He does seem like a cool kid. He seems to get along really well with the MLH kids. You guys were upstairs with them for a while."

"Chris gets along with everyone," Lisa said. "He's got the full package. Although, I wish he didn't smoke."

"Smoke? He doesn't seem like someone who would smoke," Andy said. "Does he smoke like me and Jeff, or does he smoke for real?"

Lisa rolled her eyes. "Stop bringing up Jeff!"

Andy laughed. "I'm not trying to. I'm just saying there's a huge difference between someone who has tried smoking and someone who habitually smokes. Even though you give us a ton of crap, you know Jeff and I don't smoke."

"I know you guys don't, but I don't know what Chris's deal is," Lisa said. "He didn't smoke on Saturday, but no one else did either. I think he just does it when he's around other people who do."

"I wouldn't worry about that then," Andy said. "He won't do it if he's into you and knows you don't like it."

Lisa shrugged. "I guess we'll see on Friday."

"Well, I don't know if I'll be going with you on Friday," Andy said, stopping in front of Lisa's homeroom. "If Chantal lets me, I'd like to go with her to youth group."

Lisa let out a short laugh. "And she hasn't changed you?"

Andy shrugged. "Some people just have a way of bringing out the best in others."

"Riiiiiiiight," Lisa said slowly. "Okay, thanks for the escort. See ya in math!"

"See ya," Andy said and headed off toward his homeroom.

CHAPTER 29

"Are you going to eat that piece of pizza, or just stare at it 'til next period?" Chris asked Jon during lunch on Monday.

"I'm not hungry," Jon replied.

"You're always hungry," Alyssa stated from beside Jon. "Something's bothering you."

"Chris, how was Bobby's party the other night?" Jon asked, trying to change the subject.

"I already told you that it was a good time," Chris said. "I chilled with Marc's friends most of the night."

"And Lisa, right?" Alyssa asked.

Chris smiled. "Her, too," he added.

"Are you guys going out?" Alyssa questioned Chris, widening her eyes curiously.

Chris shrugged.

"You invited her to your party, right?" Alyssa asked.

"Oh, yeah," Chris said, nodding affirmatively. "I have to take it easy on Friday, though. I have a scrimmage Saturday morning."

"Will Lisa, Leslie, and Katherine have to cheer at the scrimmage?" Alyssa asked.

"Ask them," Chris replied, nodding toward Katherine and Leslie who were sitting at the other end of the table.

"Hey, Kat and Lee! Are you guys cheering Saturday morning at Chris's scrimmage?" Alyssa called down the table.

"No," Leslie replied. "That's why I'll be able to go to Chris's on Friday."

"Oh, good," Alyssa said. "I'm glad you're going."

"I'm going for Lisa," Leslie said. "Since Chris invited her and all."

"Oh, you two are *so* going out!" Alyssa said and slapped Chris's arm. "Just admit it."

"I haven't asked her yet," Chris said.

"What are you waiting for?" Alyssa asked.

Chris shrugged.

"You should probably ask her out before you miss your chance," Jon said. "Fear paralyzes."

"Um, okay Mr. Anderson. When are you going to ask out the girl you like?" Alyssa questioned Jon, poking him in the shoulder.

"I'm not talking about it," Jon said flatly.

"You should invite her to my house Friday night," Chris said.

"I have youth group on Friday," Jon said.

"Come after," Chris suggested. "Just stay over. It won't be too crazy this time."

"Maybe I'll do that," Jon said downheartedly.

"Dude, what is eating you?" Chris asked, eyeing Jon with concern.

Jon swallowed deeply.

"Yeah, you're totally not yourself today," Alyssa stated.

Jon glanced from Alyssa to Chris, wondering if he should open up to them. After all, they were his closest friends. Since Chris had attended Bobby's party, and Alyssa had most likely heard about it from Lisa, Jon did not have the luxury of being vague.

After church on Sunday, Cathy had told Jon that Chantal had gotten sick at Bobby's party. She said that Andy had gotten Chantal drunk off spiked punch. The thought of Chantal drinking was enough to make Jon sick to his stomach. He was more confused about Chantal than he had ever been about anyone. Why would she go out with a non-believer? Why would God point out Chantal to Jon if she were dating someone else? Had he waited too long to act on what God had shown him? Should he tell her how he feels even though she's with Andy? Seeing Chantal with Andy at youth group had been painful enough to make Jon not want to go back there. Jon found himself somewhat angry at Chantal for not waiting for him. He also felt some bitterness toward God. Why would God allow him to like someone who was with someone else? Could Jon have misunderstood God?

Jon wanted to ask Chris about Chantal and Andy's interaction at the party, but he knew that would give away the identity of the girl he liked. He wanted Chantal to be the first one to know. He realized that telling her could land him in the middle of a fight with Andy. Jon sighed, hating the confusion and fear of the future that was plaguing his mind.

"You and Sartelli are both ridiculous with girls," Chris commented. "You guys act like I'd try to steal them from you or something."

"I don't know Bryan's deal, but you wouldn't be interested in the girl I'm into," Jon said. "She's way too pure."

"Speaking of pure," Chris said with a short laugh, "I saw one of your church friends at Bobby's on Saturday."

Jon locked his eyes on Chris.

"I think her boyfriend forgot to tell her that the punch had vodka in it," Chris continued. "She drank a bunch of it and got completely trashed."

"One of my friends?" Jon asked.

Chris nodded. "Cathy's sister, Chantal," he replied. "She's dating Lisa's best friend, Andy."

Jon felt his face flush.

"She got pretty sick," Chris said. "I felt bad because I knew she had no intention of drinking. The pineapple juice masked the taste of the vodka completely, so there was no way to tell it was spiked. I got pretty buzzed off a can full of it. So, I can imagine she was hurting yesterday with a massive hangover."

Jon remained silent, struggling to come up with a tactful response.

"Sterling kids drink?" Alyssa asked.

"Not really," Chris said. "Most of the kids didn't touch the punch. I think only Lisa, Andy, Chantal, and I drank it. Andy seemed sober though. He was taking care of Chantal most of the night."

"It's funny. Our student council members wouldn't even think of drinking," Alyssa said, nodding toward a table across the cafeteria where some of the student council members were sitting. "They're goody-goodies like Jon."

Jon rolled his eyes.

"Even Leslie and Katherine wouldn't drink at your party," Alyssa added. "And they're cool."

"Alyssa, *you* didn't drink at my party," Chris stated matter-of-factly. "Jay didn't drink either. Maybe it's different at Sterling, but drinking doesn't make someone cool around here."

"That's what I'm saying," Alyssa said defensively. "It's weird that Andy drinks because he's their Class President. I always thought Class Presidents were straightedge."

Chris shrugged. "Andy just seems like someone who knows how to fit in with everybody," he said. "I like him."

"That explains why Chantal wasn't at church yesterday," Jon said. "I'd be pretty mad at Andy if I were her. That was deceptive of him to not tell her there was alcohol in the punch. Are you sure he knew?"

"Lisa said she's never made it without alcohol," Chris replied.

"That's sketchy," Alyssa stated. "Every time Lisa tells me something about Andy, I think it sounds shady. Jon, you should tell Cathy to warn Chantal about Andy."

"I'm guessing Chantal's already figured out that she can't trust him," Jon said. "I feel bad for her."

"I wonder if they'll break up," Chris said.

"I'm not sure they're even officially together," Alyssa said. "Lisa told me that Chantal was hesitant to hang out with him."

"They came to youth group together on Friday," Jon said. "I assumed they were together."

"Oh," Chris said with a smirk. "Andy went to youth group on Friday?"

Jon could feel the paranoia washing over his face. Chris smiled and looked away from him and Alyssa. Jon recalled his conversation with Chris from Saturday morning. He could tell by Chris's expression that Chris knew exactly what Jon had meant by "for me."

"What's so funny, Chris?" Alyssa asked. "I knew he went to youth group."

"Nothing. Forget it," Chris stated, wiping the playful smirk off his face. "That just reminded me of something."

Jon sighed. His cover was blown. *Chris, keep quiet*, Jon wished silently.

"Well, Jonny-boy, it will be interesting to see if Andy accepts Lisa's invite to my party or if he goes back to youth group," Chris said. "Sounds like he dug himself into a hole with his girl."

After school, Chantal stood in front of her locker, holding a white envelope in her hand. When she found the card after second period, she had recognized Andy's handwriting on the envelope. Battling tears, Chantal had decided that reading the card during school would only complicate her day. She sighed. The locker hall was completely empty. There were no more classes to rush to. Any tears that seeped out of her eyes would go unnoticed. With that thought, Chantal ripped open the envelope and pulled out the card. There was a golden retriever with its tail between its legs on the cover with the words, "I'm Sorry," printed at the top. Chantal took a deep breath and opened the card:

Chantal,

If you are reading this right now, then you are being very gracious. I know I don't deserve a moment of your time. I messed up—big time. When you asked me what was in the punch, I froze. I was so scared to tell you that there was alcohol in it because I didn't want you to misjudge my friends. They're not crazy party-animals. Most of them will not go near the punch. I'm the fool who has to give everything a shot. My open-mindedness can be a blessing and a curse. I respect your morals and values. Spending time with you makes me want to be a better person. I enjoyed learning about God with you at youth group. I want to know why you are the way you are. There is something special inside of you. I can't put my finger on what it is, but whatever it is, I'm captivated by it. Please accept my apology, Chantal. I'm pretty sure I lost my chance of going out with you, but I'm hoping that somehow we can be friends. Am I crazy to have that hope? Take all the time you need to think things through. When you're ready, I'll be there with open arms, waiting to hear your voice. I mean every one of these words.
– Andy

CHAPTER 30

Monday evening, Chantal tucked herself away in her bedroom. Her inner peace was gone, and she knew that meant she needed to connect with God. Only He could give her the peace and contentment her heart desperately needed. She sat on her bed and grabbed her prayer journal off her nightstand. She chewed on the end of her pen's cap and stared at a blank page inside the journal. After a moment she began writing:

Dear Lord,

I have noticed that the areas in life I concern myself with the least always seem to work out just fine. The areas I fret over and think about constantly always seem to be complicated messes. I had a realization. When I concern myself, over-analyze, and fret, I am doing what the Bible says will only cause harm. When I don't worry about something, I trust You to handle it in Your perfect way. When I fret, I show a lack of faith. I'm so sorry. I need to turn some things over to You. I give You every thought of Jon. I give You every thought of Andy. I give you the entire boy-department of my life. Like every other department, I know You have that one under control. Please keep my mind on what is real and true. Worrying about the future is unproductive. It is not real or true. I am taking my hands

off all my relationships with guys and praying for You to open and close whatever doors You'd like. I accept that You withhold no good thing from anyone who walks with You. May Your will be done. I am learning that it is in the art of letting go and accepting all You send my way that I find contentment, strength, and peace. Thank You.
I pray this all in Jesus' name,
Chantal

***

Monday night, Jon was lying on his bed, staring blankly at his ceiling fan, when he heard two loud knocks on this bedroom door. "Come in," he called out, without taking his eyes off the ceiling.

"Snap out of this daze, Anderson," Chris said as he entered Jon's bedroom. He sat down at Jon's desk, and spun around to face the bed. "Talk to me."

"Huh?" Jon asked, sitting up straight.

"You like Chantal," Chris said flatly, "and she thinks you like her sister."

"What?" Jon asked.

Chris nodded. "Yeah. Chantal, Andy, Lisa, Alyssa—they all think you're into Cathy. Cathy might even think you're into her."

"That's crazy!" Jon exclaimed, lowering his eyebrows and his jaw. "Why would Chantal think I like Cathy? I like Cathy as a friend, but not as a girlfriend. Chantal's sweet, gentle, and outgoing. She's perfect. Why wouldn't I like her?"

Chris laughed. "Well, I made it clear to Andy and Lisa that you're not dating Cathy. They seemed pretty adamant that you were. I'm just telling you this so you can set things straight with Chantal. I think what happened Saturday night between Andy and Chantal might have been a gift to you from God. You're getting a second chance. There's no way she's going to date him now. And you know, she might have only dated him because she thought you liked her sister," he suggested. "She could like you, dude."

"Why would people think I'm into *Cathy*?" Jon asked.

"I don't know," Chris said with a shrug. "I don't know her. Chantal's pretty cute though, so Cathy must be, too."

"Chantal's beautiful," Jon corrected him. "Cathy's pretty, but there's something much more attractive to me about Chantal."

"Go after her, dude," Chris said matter-of-factly. "Call her right now and tell her what you just told me."

"I can't do that!" Jon exclaimed, turning red at the thought.

"Wait, who's the guy that told me to ask Lisa out before it's too late?" Chris asked, smirking at Jon expectantly.

Jon let out a heavy breath.

"Dude, you've been saying forever that you're not going to be into a girl unless you know she's the right one," Chris said. "So, you must think Chantal is the right one. I don't understand what's stopping you from pursuing her?"

"Well, I think I should give her time to get over Andy," Jon replied quickly.

"Really?!" Chris asked sarcastically.

"I don't know," Jon stated. "I'll figure it out by the weekend."

"Are you coming over Friday?" Chris asked. "There's going to be a lot more college kids there this time. I'm only inviting a few of our friends. Taylor's really the one dominating the party. MLH has a big game on Saturday, so Jordan put a dry-band on the players."

"Jordan, dry?" Jon questioned him. "As in, not drinking?"

Chris laughed. "That's what he said, but we'll see what happens."

"I think I'm going to come," Jon said. "This is the first time I've ever wanted to skip youth group."

"That's kind of weird," Chris stated, raising one eyebrow skeptically.

"Well, I don't want to see Chantal with Andy," Jon commented.

"Anderson, if you tell Chantal how you feel, then she could be with *you* at youth group," Chris reasoned. "Can't you pray for courage, or something?" he added with a short laugh.

CHAPTER 31

Dear Andy,

I know you'd rather hear this in person, but I'm much better at penning my thoughts on paper. I'm sorry it has taken me two days to get back to you. I accept your apology and forgive you. I'm glad you enjoyed learning about God, and I think it's really cool that you see something special in me. I know what you see is Christ alive inside of me. I hope someday you know what I mean by that.

You say you're sure you lost your chance with me but hope that we can be friends. I say you never know what the future will bring. I know right now I need to be spending time with people who share my faith. I need friends who can encourage me to pray, trust, and seek God's guidance. If you really enjoyed youth group and have curiosity about God, I encourage you to seek Him. Try to figure out what you believe and why you believe it. Ask God to reveal Himself to you. Pick up the Bible and read about Him. It's impossible to recognize someone if you don't know what they look like. You won't be able to see God at work in your life unless you know what He's like. I think God could use you for a lot of good, and He could even have a plan for you and me down the road. The only way I see us ever

getting close again is if we share the bond of Christ. You've got to figure this all out for yourself. I've enjoyed getting to know you.
Your friend,
Chantal

Chantal,

Don't worry about taking two days! You could have taken two years, and I still would have been happy to hear from you. I respect everything you wrote and want to thank you for being so open and forgiving. I would like to try youth group with you again sometime. Maybe I could get Lisa or Bobby to go with me. You never know! I'm glad we can be friends, and I'm glad you are open to the possibility of us one day getting closer. You have inspired me to look for a deeper meaning in life. I hope I find it because I'd love to have the vibrancy I see in you.
Enjoy the rest of the week,
Andy

*****

Friday afternoon, Lisa waited by Chantal and Cathy's lockers. After a few moments of waiting, Lisa saw Cathy heading toward her. Lisa swallowed deeply and stared at Cathy until she was only a few feet away.

"Are you waiting for someone?" Cathy questioned Lisa as she stepped up to her locker. Cathy did not glance in Lisa's direction as she turned her combination lock.

"I wanted to invite you and Chantal to my friend's party tonight," Lisa replied.

"What a great idea," Cathy sang sarcastically. "If I'm lucky I might end up puking for the next two days like my sister did last weekend."

Lisa rolled her eyes. "None of us meant for that to happen," she said. "We all like Chantal a lot. Andy's really broken up about the whole situation."

"Well, you live and learn," Cathy shrugged carelessly as she peered inside her locker.

"Besides," Lisa continued, "the party is at Chris Dunkin's house. I thought Jon Anderson might have invited you already."

Cathy looked up from her science binder and glanced at Lisa.

"You and Jon are tight, right?" Lisa pressed, eyeing Cathy expectantly.

Cathy squinted at Lisa suspiciously.

"Okay, regardless," Lisa stated abruptly. "Chris and I are kind of a thing now, and he said I could invite anyone I want to his house. So, you and Chantal should think of coming by."

"Is Andy going?" Cathy asked.

"Maybe," Lisa replied. "Why, are you still that mad at him?"

Cathy cocked her head to the side and stared hard at Lisa.

Lisa sighed. "I know you never liked him to begin with, but I'm surprised you are holding such a grudge. Isn't forgiveness part of your Christian creed?"

"Andy apologized to Chantal, and she forgave him," Cathy said flatly. "Yes, forgiveness is part of my 'creed,' but it doesn't mean I have to hang out with Andy. I believe in fleeing from temptation and spending my time productively. So, that would rule out Chris's party. I only asked if Andy was going because I was trying to figure out why you invited Chantal and me."

"You have such a suspicious mind," Lisa said, shaking her head. "Do you trust anyone?"

"I trust myself," Cathy replied. "I trust my instincts enough to believe you have an ulterior motive for inviting us. I don't dislike you for it, but I'd rather you just tell me the truth."

Lisa let out a short breath and crossed her arms. "Every time I'm nice to you I end up regretting it. You're right. Andy asked me to invite Chantal—but I decided to invite both of you."

"Well, thank you for proving my instincts right and thank you for inviting me," Cathy said, turning back toward her locker. "I'm going to youth group tonight, but maybe we can hang out another time."

Lisa laughed. "You mean sometime when Andy and Chantal aren't involved?"

"You got it," Cathy sang and shut her locker. "I'll tell Chantal about Chris's party, but there's no way she'll be interested. Even if I didn't tell her Andy was going, she would still keep her distance."

"He really does like her, you know," Lisa stated earnestly. "I've never seen him fall that hard for anyone."

"I don't question that he likes her," Cathy said. "I just know that if a guy is going to capture Chantal's heart, then God's going to have to capture his heart first."

"Is that why you like Jon?" Lisa asked. "Because he loves God like you do?"

"What makes you think I like Jon?" Cathy asked, lowering her eyebrows and staring at Lisa curiously.

"I just heard you guys were close, that's all," Lisa replied. "Maybe from Chris, or Chantal, or someone."

"We're friends," Cathy stated flatly.

"All right!" Lisa cried defensively. "Remind me never to ask you about a boy again."

"It would take a very feisty boy to put up with me," Cathy said and laughed.

Lisa lowered her eyebrows. "Hmmm. I may know one," she said.

CHAPTER 32

At youth group on Friday night, Chantal's heart skipped a beat whenever she heard footsteps coming down the corridor. Every time the door swung open, her eyes grew wide and her stomach dropped. After Jessie finished singing, Chantal took one last glance at the closed door. Then, she gave up all hope of seeing Jon that night.

"Come in!" Chris greeted Lisa, Leslie, and Alyssa as he opened his front door. "I'm glad you girls could make it."

"Hi!" Lisa exclaimed and threw her arms around Chris. "Andy and Bobby are on their way. Thanks for letting me invite my friends."

Chris laughed. "Anytime."

"Wow, a lot of your cousins' friends are here," Alyssa said, shooting her hazel eyes around the living room. "Who else is coming that's our age?"

"Jay and Bryan are on their way," Chris replied, shutting the door behind the girls. "Jon is, too. I didn't invite anyone else. I have to make tonight an early night because of my scrimmage tomorrow."

"Wow, Jon's skipping youth group?" Alyssa questioned Chris. "He's seriously not himself this week."

Chris shrugged. "Let me get you guys drinks," he said, purposely changing the subject. "Uh, I hope you girls like soda because Jordan put a dry-band on the football team, and Taylor hasn't tapped the keg yet."

"Soda works," Lisa said as she, Leslie, and Alyssa followed Chris into the kitchen.

"Hi, Lisa. Hi, girls," Marc greeted them as he leaned against the granite kitchen counter.

"Hi," the girls replied in unison as they smiled at Marc.

"So, help yourself," Chris said, opening the refrigerator door. "We can hang out in my room or stay downstairs until everyone else gets here. It's up to you guys."

"I don't care," Lisa replied, taking cans of soda out of the fridge and passing them to Leslie and Alyssa.

"Where's Katie?" Alyssa asked, referring to Chris's little sister.

"She's with my parents," Marc stated, perching himself up on the counter. "She doesn't need to witness the stuff that goes on here when Taylor's in charge."

"Where *is* Taylor?" Chris asked.

"He had to pick some people up at the train station," Marc replied. "A bunch of his college friends are staying for the weekend."

"Why not? I mean, this house is more like a frat than a family home anyway," Chris stated sarcastically and rolled his eyes.

Marc's cell phone began ringing, and he answered it with great speed. "Hey, are you here?" he called into the phone. "Okay, I'll be right out."

"That was definitely a girl," Chris said quietly to Lisa, Alyssa, and Leslie, as he watched Marc rush out of the kitchen. The girls laughed. "So, do you guys want to head to the family room? Once Taylor gets back with his friends and Jordan's friends start showing up, there's not going to be much room to—"

"—N-U! N-U! N-U!" a loud chant erupted, masking the rest of Chris's sentence, as Taylor and a train of college kids barged through the side door into the kitchen.

"Let the fun begin," Chris said and winked at Lisa.

At eight o'clock, Andy and Bobby were walking through the streets of Montgomery on their way to Chris's house. "I don't know what to expect tonight," Andy said to Bobby. "Lisa said Chris's older cousins were the ones throwing the party."

"The Dunkins are animals," Bobby stated flatly. "Marc's somewhat normal, but the rest of them are insane."

"Marc's friends with my brother," Andy said, "and I think Chris seems cool."

"Yeah, okay buddy, then let's start with Jordan," Bobby began in an amused manner. "Rumor has it that last year he stole the captain of AHS's football team's car, drove on the AHS field, tore it up by doing donuts, and left the car parked in the end zone."

Andy widened his eyes. "What?" he questioned Bobby, letting out a short laugh.

"And he didn't get caught," Bobby added. "Now, let's talk about Taylor. Taylor was ranked by ESPN as one of the top 100 college football recruits in the country. He's a Montgomery legend. Here's the thing, though: Taylor parties as hard as he plays ball. During his senior year at MLH, Taylor got arrested for streaking with the Varsity cheerleaders. He's absolutely insane."

"Woah, dude," Andy laughed. "And Chris's parents leave Jordan and Taylor to babysit their kids?"

"Yup, which is exactly why we are on our way to a party," Bobby stated dryly. "Lisa's fallen for a kid who's trying to live up to the Dunkin legacy. If she goes out with him, then she's going to see some crazy things."

"Yeah, like Jeff have a heart attack?" Andy joked. "I feel bad for him, bro. We should meet up with him later on. I agreed to come for Lis, but Jeff's our boy. We can't ditch him for his competition."

"Touché," Bobby said. "All right, we'll stay long enough to make sure Lis and her friends are okay; then we'll bounce."

"I still don't understand why her cheerleading friends will go to Chris's parties and not any of ours," Andy said.

"Dude, those girls are from the Lake. They grew up with Chris and his friends," Bobby commented matter-of-factly. "But tonight is our chance to buddy up with them."

"Point well taken," Andy laughed.

CHAPTER 33

Jon glanced at his bedroom clock. Youth group was already well on its way, if not almost over. He sighed, realizing he should have gone. Chris's party was supposed to be his scapegoat, yet he hadn't even scrounged up enough motivation to leave his bedroom. As he sat up on his bed, he began wondering how his affection for Chantal had turned so paralytic.

Ten minutes later, with nothing but images of Chantal dancing through his mind, Jon stepped down his front steps. He glanced at his driveway, at the exact spot where God had revealed His will to Jon. Jon remembered how the vision of Chantal and him together had sent him to the pavement in awe. As he trudged past that spot on his driveway and made way to his street, Jon realized he had let fear hinder his faith. After guarding his heart for so long, he had been afraid to make himself vulnerable by opening up his heart to Chantal. Now, he was just miserable.

"Taylor tapped the keg," Chris said to Lisa as they stood by his dining room table. "Do you want me to get you a beer?"

"Are you going to drink?" Lisa asked.

Chris shook his head. "No, I have a game in the morning," he replied. "I'm fine with you drinking even though I'm not. It's completely up to you."

Lisa realized she was seeing a different side of Chris. He had no agenda to liven up the party or to show off. Instead, he was acting like the focused athlete Alyssa had once described to her. Seeing this side of Chris made Lisa feel even more attracted to him. "I'm fine with soda," she replied.

"That's not the Lisa I know," Chris teased her while pulling on a strand of her dark hair.

Lisa shrugged. "Andy made a good point the other day. He said that he knew how to have a lot of fun before he ever took a sip of alcohol," she said. "So, I'm thinking that if you're really as fun as I think you are, then I shouldn't need to drink in order to have a good time with you."

"You're right," Chris agreed. "I might not be as wild as usual, but I'm still a whole lot of fun."

"Oh really?" Lisa challenged him. "Well, then tell me, Christopher, can you dance?"

"Dance?! You want the star wide receiver of Montgomery Lake Midget football to dance?!" Chris exclaimed with a short laugh.

Lisa smiled and nodded expectantly.

"Well, then it's your lucky day," Chris said, winking at Lisa as he pulled her out of the dining room and into the family room.

The family room was filled with MLH kids. Of course, Jordan was in the center of the craze, cutting up a rug with Michelle Taylor. Lisa watched in amazement at how loosely and quickly Michelle's body was moving to the fast beat of the top-forty music. The girl was beautiful, to say the least, and an incredible dancer. Jordan had stripped down to his wife beater, showing off his enormous biceps, and he was having no problem keeping pace with Michelle.

Chris took Lisa's hand and twirled her into the center of the high school kids' circle without hesitation.

"Little D!" Jordan exclaimed, patting Chris on the shoulder. "Show 'em what you got!"

Chris paused for a split second and then laughed. "Hold up! Hold up!" he yelled, making his way through the crowd to the iPod dock. "You got any Britney Spears on here?"

Lisa dropped her jaw. She could not tell if Chris was being serious, or if he was trying to be funny. Her answer came five seconds later when *Oops!...I Did It Again* began blaring from the surround sound.

"Omigod do you remember this?!" Jordan suddenly exclaimed, clapping his hands together and laughing hysterically. "Marky-Marc get over here! Little D! You're the man! Haaaaha!"

Lisa widened her eyes as all of the high school kids around her began laughing hysterically and clapping. Clearly they knew something she didn't.

"Is that what I think it is?" Marc shouted, pulling his shirt over his head and rushing into circle.

"Oh, yeah!" Jordan yelled.

Lisa could not believe her eyes. Jordan, Marc, and Chris were, with straight faces, about to perform a Britney Spears concert for the room full of teenagers.

"Woah, Little D's got some muscles!" one of the cheerleaders yelled as Chris tore off his shirt.

Lisa covered her mouth in awe of what was taking place. The Dunkins—"guy's-guys"—were before her eyes, half naked, singing their hearts out to old-school Britney. Lisa laughed hysterically as Chris, shamelessly, danced like a girl amidst the crowd of MLH kids. They loved him.

"Wooo! Yaaaa Dunkin!" Jason yelled as he appeared beside Lisa. "They did this last year at the football fundraiser," he said to Lisa. "They won first place."

"I can see why," Lisa said with a laugh.

"All right, screw dry-band!" Jordan yelled at the completion of the song. "Keg stands in the kitchen!"

Chris rolled his eyes at his cousin and walked over to Lisa. "I am *not* doing a keg stand," he whispered to Lisa, shaking his head from side to side.

"Little D! You're doing a keg stand with me!" Jordan exclaimed, locking his arm around Chris's head.

"Oh, crap, yes I am!" Chris yelled to Lisa as Jordan carried him off into the kitchen. Lisa laughed and followed the crowd as it made way to the next main event.

"Michelle, watch out," one of the MLH girls said as she stopped Michelle from falling into Lisa. "Sorry," the girl said to Lisa. "She must have had too much to drink."

"Woah, thanks, Katie," Michelle said, attempting to stand up straight. "I don't feel so well."

"Do you want to go lie down?" the girl named Katie asked

Michelle. "Maybe Jordan can take you to Chris's room or something? You should try to sleep for a little while."

"Will you ask him for me?" Michelle asked, slurring a few of her words.

"Yeah, wait here," Katie replied. "Ally! Wait here with Michelle! I have to go get Jordan or Marc," she yelled to a nearby girl. Lisa watched as the girl named Ally rushed to Michelle's side. Lisa didn't mean to eavesdrop, but she was pinned beside them in the crowd. She observed the concerned look on Ally's face as she looked into Michelle's eyes.

"Shells, are you all right?" Ally asked. "Your eyes don't look right to me. What did you drink?"

"Diet Pepsi… some water… I don't know," Michelle replied lethargically.

Lisa shot her eyes to the floor when Ally glanced over at her.

"Excuse me, excuse me," Jordan shouted, pushing his way toward Michelle. "What's going on? What's wrong, Michelle?"

"I think she needs to go lie down," Ally said, looking up at Jordan. Jordan's usually cocky disposition appeared somber as he glanced at Michelle. Lisa watched, wondering if Jordan had a nurturing bone in his well-built body or if he was going to leave Michelle in her friends' care.

"I'm going to be sick," Michelle stated, grabbing hold of her stomach.

"All right, let's get to the bathroom," Jordan said, taking hold of Michelle and steadying her body against his. "I'll take care of her, girls. Go enjoy the party."

Ally and Katie glanced from Jordan to each other, looking somewhat skeptical. Without saying another word, Jordan led Michelle off toward the bathroom.

"Do you trust him with her?" Ally asked Katie.

"I don't know," Katie replied uneasily. "Let's go tell Marc what's going on. He'll know what to do."

Ally nodded. "Excuse us," she said, pushing past Lisa toward the kitchen. Lisa stepped aside, allowing both girls to pass by.

"Hey!" Chris said as he tapped Lisa on the shoulder. "Sorry about that. Jordan gets a little caught up in the moment sometimes. I knew his dry-band wouldn't last."

"And you thought you'd escape without drinking tonight?" Lisa said, putting her arms around Chris and smiling at him.

"One thirty-second keg stand won't kill me," Chris said with a smirk. "Although, I might be sore in the morning from my sick dance moves."

Lisa laughed.

"So, you still like me sober?" Chris asked playfully, looking into Lisa's eyes.

"Maybe even better," Lisa replied before bringing her lips to meet his.

"Nice," Chris said, pulling Lisa in closely and kissing her gently. He ran his hand through her hair and then brushed her cheek with his thumb. "I like you, too."

Lisa held her green eyes on him steadily.

"Would it be too cliché for the hottest cheerleader on the A-squad to go out with the captain of the football team?" Chris asked facetiously.

Lisa lowered her eyebrows and laughed. "What is it with you Dunkins and hot cheerleaders?"

Chris shrugged. "We just have good taste," he replied.

"Well, I don't think it would be too cliché," Lisa stated and shook her head. "When the captain of the football team dances around his house to Britney Spears, I don't think anything could be cliché!" she exclaimed.

"Then that settles it," Chris said, taking Lisa's hand. "You're my girlfriend."

Lisa shrugged. "All right then," she agreed with a smile, "it's settled."

Jon's heart pounded heavily against his chest as he opened Chris's front door. He had walked through that door thousands of times before, but never during one of Taylor's "ragers." As Jon stepped into Chris's living room, the odor of beer besieged his nostrils. Chris's home—the normally calm spot, perfect for watching Patriots games—resembled a whirlwind.

"Anderson!" Jason hollered from the hallway adjacent to the living room. Jason began making his way through the sea of college kids—Taylor's friends. "Dude, this is ill," Jason stated, cupping his right hand with Jon's and patting him on the back. "Chris just did a thirty-second keg stand, and Sartelli shotgunned a beer with Taylor."

Jon widened his eyes. He hated the words that had just flown out of his friend's mouth. *Chris drinking, again?! Even though he has a game tomorrow?* Jon sighed.

"Don't be scarrrrrred," Jason sang, laughing and pushing Jon further into the party. "I'm staying sober tonight, too, buddy."

"I have to use the bathroom," Jon said, breaking free from Jason. He pushed through the crowd, thinking that, as a seventh grader, he must look like an infant to the majority of the partiers. After elbowing his way to the bathroom, Jon knocked loudly on the closed door. He knocked three times before he received a response.

"Hold on!" Jordan's distinct voice rang back. A moment later, the bathroom door swung open with great force. Jon's eyes collided with the glassy blue eyes of Montgomery Lake High's Varsity football captain.

"Oh! Jonny A! What's up, buddy?" Jordan laughed, patting Jon on the shoulder. "Sorry about that, buddy. My friend here's not feeling so hot," he added, referring to the disheveled but beautiful brunette leaning against his right side.

"No problem," Jon said, observing the nauseated look on the girl's face as he stepped past her. *What am I doing here? This was a huge mistake,* he thought.

Stepping back into the chaos of the party a moment later, Jon's attention was immediately stolen away. "Get away from her!" Marc's angry voice echoed through the party. "Jordan!" he screamed, flying up the nearby staircase after his older brother without hesitation. The sound of Marc's feet hitting each step domineered the chant of the party. Jon rushed to the bottom of the stairs. Jason, Chris, and Bryan joined him within seconds.

"Oh crap," Chris huffed, watching his older cousins with a look of horror on his face. "Not good."

"Jordan! Get out of the room!" Marc demanded, angrily banging on Chris's bedroom door at the top of the stairs.

Chris's eyes widened. "He's going to break my door down!"

"Who's in there with Jordan?" Jason asked.

Jon watched as Marc, in one fluid motion, threw his five-foot-eleven, one-hundred-eighty-five-pound, muscular body against the door.

From beside Jon, Chris began pushing through the large crowd gathered at the bottom of the stairs. "Marc, hold up!" he called, running up the stairs toward his irate cousin. "Who is he in there with?"

"Do you have a key?" Marc asked Chris frantically as he leaned his weight fully against the door. "Jordan, get away from her!"

From the bottom of the stairs, Jon was unable to decipher Chris's response.

"He's going to rape her!" Marc screamed as he kicked the door.

Jon watched in horror. *Oh no. The girl from the bathroom,* he thought. He panicked, racking his brain for a way to help.

"Open the door, J!" Chris shouted.

Jon watched, frozen, as Marc and Chris continued kicking the door until it became loose on its hinges. Before the door completely broke open, Jordan whipped it open.

Sweat trickled from Jon's forehead as he watched Jordan slam Marc against the wall. Marc wrestled Jordan to the ground and pinned him down by the top step. Jon saw Chris take one look at his cousins and then disappear into his bedroom.

"What is wrong with you?!" Jordan yelled, trying to push his way free. "You're insane!"

"Don't touch her!" Marc screamed. "What did you put in her drink?!"

"What are you talking about?" Jordan asked in a strained voice as he out-maneuvered Marc with little effort.

"Woah! Woah! Woah!" Taylor exclaimed, pushing past Jon and the crowd gathered at the bottom of the stairs. "Break it up!" he shouted, hustling up the stairs to reach his dueling younger brothers. Taylor separated Jordan and Marc with little effort. "Are you trying to ruin my party? Do you want to get arrested? What the heck is wrong with you?!" he yelled in Marc's face.

"He drugged Michelle!" Marc exclaimed, pushing past Taylor toward Chris's bedroom. "Chris, let me in!" he cried, banging on the door. A moment later, Marc disappeared into the bedroom.

Jon watched as Taylor yanked Jordan into the upstairs bathroom and slammed the door shut.

"That's messed up," Jason said, turning toward Jon. He looked ghostly pale. "That's Kristen's sister."

"Where's Kristen?" Jon asked.

"Grounded."

"Because of what happened between you two?"

"No. There's no way her parents found out about *that*," Jason stated confidently. "Should we leave?"

"I don't feel right staying," Jon replied.

"Sartelli, do you want to bounce?" Jason called to Bryan, who was leaning against the nearby living room couch.

"Sup?" Bryan yelled over the roar of the party that had returned to its normal volume. It seemed to Jon as if most of the partiers were unshaken by the confrontation that had just taken place. *God help me to never become that desensitized,* he thought.

"Do you want to head out?" Jason asked, stepping toward Bryan. "We can go to my house."

Bryan nodded. "I'm really glad I didn't invite Courtney here. What a freakin' disaster."

"I can't believe Chris has to deal with this crap every time his parents go away," Jon stated. "Thank God for Marc."

"I don't know how Marc's related to Taylor or Jordan," Jason said. "If they weren't all amazing football players, I would think Marc was adopted."

"I have to get out of here," Jon said.

"We're right behind you, man," Jason said, patting Jon on the shoulders.

Once inside Chris's room, Marc slammed the door, locked it, and pulled a nearby table in front of it.

"She's sleeping," Chris said from the side of his bed.

Marc's heart pounded. *Please be fully clothed. Please be fully clothed,* he thought as he walked over to the bed. The blankets were covering Michelle's frail body. Her hair was tussled, her face was sickly pale, and her breathing was deep. "Chris, look the other way," he said, taking hold of the comforter. Slowly, he began pulling it back, revealing Michelle's bare body, inch by inch. His heart seemed to jump into his throat. He threw the covers back over her, turned away from the bed, and began dry heaving.

"What's wrong?" Chris asked.

Marc looked up at his younger cousin, and then buried his head in his hands as he sat down on the bed. "How did I let this happen?" Marc felt tears begin to well up inside his eyes. He loved Michelle. Love protects. *Love always protects!* How had he allowed Jordan to do this?

"Is she all right?" Chris asked.

Marc swallowed the large lump in his throat and glanced up at Chris. "Will you grab me one of your t-shirts?"

Chris nodded and retrieved a shirt from his bureau.

"Just guard the door," Marc said as he took the shirt from Chris. "I have to get her dressed." As Marc pulled the covers off of Michelle, he tried not to lust after her body. Tussled, mangled, and sick, Michelle was still the most beautiful girl Marc had ever seen. As he lifted her up against the headboard, he let out a loud sigh of relief. "Thank God, thank God, thank God," he said, resting his forehead against hers. "We made it in time," he said as he pulled Chris's shirt over Michelle's head.

"We did?" Chris asked from the doorway. "You mean, she isn't naked?"

Marc shook his head and laid Michelle back down on Chris's bed. "Her leggings and skirt are still perfectly intact," he said happily, gently placing the covers on top of her.

"Marc?" Michelle asked quietly, without opening her eyes.

"Hey, yeah," Marc said softly, kneeling down beside the bed so that he was eyelevel with her.

"Thanks," she murmured.

"I'm going to stay right here, with you, all night," Marc said. "You're safe, Shells."

Jon stepped onto Chris's side porch with Bryan and Jason. The brisk fall air slapped him in the face as he noticed Leslie, leaning against an athletically built boy with spiked black hair.

"Sup, Leslie?" Jason called as he kicked her in the butt playfully. "You just missed one hell of a scene."

"Hi, guys," Leslie said, turning around to face the boys. "What happened?"

When the boy with his arm around Leslie turned around, Jon felt the color drain from his face. *Andy.*

"Oh, hey, Jon," Andy said. "I met you last week at youth group. You're going out with Chantal's sister, right?"

Jon felt fury rising up inside him. "No, I'm not going out with Cathy," he stated flatly, "and I hope you're not going out with Chantal."

Leslie turned abruptly toward Andy. "You have a girlfriend?!"

Andy locked eyes with Jon for a second. "No, I don't have a girlfriend," he said as he turned toward Leslie.

"A week ago, you were after Chantal, and now you're hanging all over Leslie?" Jon questioned Andy. "I'm sorry, I just don't get that."

"Why are you so upset, Jon? What's going on?" Leslie asked. "Who's Chantal?"

"Forget it," Jon said, shaking his head from side to side. "I'm out of here," he added as he stalked off the porch to Chris's driveway.

CHAPTER 34

"Anderson! Anderson!" Jason called out, running after Jon down Chris's street. "Anderson! Hold up, buddy!"

"He's on a mission or something," Bryan huffed as he caught up to Jason.

Jon turned around at the end of Chris's street. "I'm going for a run," he called. "I'll catch up with you guys tomorrow."

"A run? Now?" Jason asked, hustling to catch up to Jon. "You are one of the weirdest kids I have ever met."

"He always runs to let off steam," Bryan said as they neared the end of the street. "Obviously that kid with Leslie pissed him off."

"Guys, I said I'd see you tomorrow," Jon stated, sounding irritated as Jason and Bryan caught up to him.

"You're a tool-bag!" Jason exclaimed.

"Dude, where are you running to?" Bryan asked, looking at Jon like he was some sort of alien.

"Sterling," Jon replied. "I have somewhere to be before it gets too late. I have to go."

"What is it? A church thing?" Jason asked as Jon turned away from him and Bryan.

"I don't know yet," Jon called without turning around. Five seconds later he vanished from Jason and Bryan's sight into the darkness of the night.

Mrs. Kagelli picked up Chantal and Cathy from youth group at nine o'clock. As the twins hustled into the car, Mrs. Kagelli glanced at Chantal with a concerned expression. "What happened?"

"Nothing," Chantal said quietly and hung her head. "Jon wasn't there."

"Chantal, I told you that he was going to Chris Dunkin's party," Cathy stated from the backseat.

"Yeah, Jon *and* Andy," Chantal sighed and peered out her window. "That would have been a fun party to attend," she added sarcastically.

"Do you girls feel like ice cream?" Mrs. Kagelli asked brightly.

"Um, yes!" Cathy exclaimed.

Chantal shrugged.

"I think we could all use some ice cream right now," Mrs. Kagelli remarked cheerfully. "Chantal, if God wants you to talk to Jon about everything, like you think He does, then He'll open the door. God will give you an opportunity to speak with him. God's not in a rush."

"I know, Mom," Chantal said downheartedly. "I just really thought we were supposed to talk tonight. I knew about Chris's party, but I thought Jon would come to youth group first."

"Well, maybe it bothered him to see you with Andy last week," Cathy suggested. "I've already told you that he didn't seem happy. He kept looking over at you two. Then, he got really mad when I told him about what happened at Bobby's party. His reaction alone was proof that he cares a lot about you."

"Why are you saying this stuff?" Chantal questioned Cathy. "Do you actually want me to like Jon?"

"I'd rather have you like Jon than Andy!" Cathy exclaimed. "I told you weeks ago that Andy was a distraction sent by Satan. I also told you that Andy could interfere with God's plan for you and Jon. Why wouldn't I want you to like Jon?"

"I don't know, maybe because *you* like Jon!" Chantal retorted, whipping her head around to face Cathy.

"You are the second person who has told me that today," Cathy said with a laugh. "I do not like Jon!"

"Who else said that?" Chantal asked.

"Lisa," Cathy replied. "She said someone told her that I was close with him. She said it might have been you."

"I didn't say you were close with Jon. I just told her that you two were hanging out when I went to her house," Chantal said, turning back around.

"Well, whatever," Cathy said. "I don't like Jon." Silence reigned over the car for the next minute until Cathy added, "I can't believe you think I like the boy you like! Do you really think I would backstab you like that?! I've always had your back!"

"I guess I just like Jon so much that I can't understand why you wouldn't," Chantal stated after a moment of thought, keeping her eyes locked on the windshield.

"I wouldn't expect us to have the same taste in guys," Cathy laughed. "Jon's too serious in my opinion."

"I don't think he's serious," Chantal said, a bit defensively. "He's just passionate about the things he cares about. That doesn't make him serious; it makes him interesting."

"I'm glad you see it that way," Cathy said, "but I don't."

"You really don't like Jon?" Chantal asked, turning around to gaze at Cathy.

"I *really* don't."

"And you don't think he likes you?"

"I'm pretty sure Jon treats me like he treats everyone else," Cathy replied. "He's friendly but not flirty. If he likes me, then I'm oblivious."

"Wow," Chantal said, turning to look at her mother. "Fear and jealousy got the best of me."

Twenty minutes later, Chantal was sitting in the front seat of her mother's car, licking her coffee ice cream, when her heart froze in her chest. Suddenly, her hand let go of the cone, and her ice cream bounced off her lap onto the floormat. "What the heck is *Jon* doing here?!" she screamed, oblivious to the ice cream smeared across her jeans.

"I don't know," Mrs. Kagelli concluded slowly as she steered the car into their driveway.

"Oh my gosh, am I bright red?" Chantal asked frantically.

"Chantal, calm down!" Cathy cried. "He is going to see you freaking out."

"I'm shaking," Chantal said. "Maybe he's here to talk to you!"

"Didn't we just go over that?"

Instead of pulling the car into the garage, Mrs. Kagelli stopped in the driveway. "Chantal, go meet Jon on the steps," she said. "Go on."

"What if he's not here for me?" Chantal asked. "Oh my gosh! I have ice cream all over my lap! Do you have a napkin?"

Cathy laughed at Chantal. "I'll go greet Jon," she said, rolling her eyes. "Clean yourself up."

Mrs. Kagelli parked the car in the garage and looked over at Chantal. "You look like you are about to throw up," she said. "Relax."

Chantal nodded and opened her door. "He's probably here to talk to Cathy," she said quietly. "I swear he likes her." She followed her mom up the garage stairs.

"What are you doing?" Mrs. Kagelli asked. "Go see what Jon wants."

"Isn't Cathy taking care of that?"

Mrs. Kagelli peered at Chantal expectantly.

"Mom, don't shut the garage!" Cathy called from out of sight. "We're coming in that way."

Chantal's heart began to race. She turned toward the garage door and saw Jon hustling through it behind Cathy. By the time Jon reached the stairs, Chantal's palms were drenched with sweat.

"Hi, Mrs. Kagelli," Jon said. "I'm sorry to come over so late, and so unexpectedly… I… um… wasn't at youth group tonight, and there's something I need to tell Chantal."

Chantal's eyes widened as Cathy stood beside Jon and smiled. Chantal could tell from Cathy's expression that she was trying her best not to laugh.

"Come on inside, Jon," Mrs. Kagelli said as she unlocked the door. "Did you run here?"

"Yes, I did," Jon replied, following Chantal inside the house.

"Let me get you some water then," Mrs. Kagelli said, leading everyone into the kitchen. "Would you like a snack as well?"

"No thanks. Water's good, though," Jon answered.

"I'm going up to my room," Cathy said, glancing from Chantal to Jon. "Good night. Nice to see you, Jon."

"Good night," Chantal, Jon, and Mrs. Kagelli said in unison.

"Chantal, grab Jon a glass of water. I'm going to leave you guys alone," Mrs. Kagelli said. "I'll be upstairs if you need me."

"Thanks for letting me in, Mrs. Kagelli," Jon said.

Mrs. Kagelli smiled warmly at Jon and then walked out of the kitchen.

"What are you doing here?" Chantal asked while handing Jon a glass of water and leading him over to the kitchen table.

Jon let out a heavy breath. His face slowly began to turn red as he took a seat at the table. Chantal peered at him expectantly. "Well, um, okay," he stammered. "Tonight, I went to Chris's party instead of going to youth group."

"Okay."

"I didn't even want to go, but I went anyway," Jon continued. "I never should have skipped youth group for that party. It was horrible. Some girl almost got raped, and Chris's cousins got in a fight with each other. The whole thing was a mess."

"Yikes!"

"Your friend—I hope *not* your boyfriend—Andy was at the party," Jon said, looking Chantal in the eye. "He was outside with my friend Leslie, and he seemed kind of into her."

At the sound of those words, Chantal dropped her eyes and fidgeted uncomfortably in her seat.

"I hope he's not your boyfriend," Jon added.

"Is that why you came here?" Chantal asked. "To tell me that Andy was flirting with your friend?"

"No," Jon laughed, "that's definitely *not* why I came here."

"Oh, okay," Chantal said with relief. "Well, Andy's not my boyfriend. We're friends. He liked me, but he was never my boyfriend."

"Good," Jon said with a nod. "I could see how into you he was at youth group last week, and it bothered me to see him put his arm around Leslie. I don't know what is between you and him, but I wanted to make sure you were okay."

"There's nothing between Andy and me," Chantal assured him. "I thought there was a chance of us becoming something, but after I got to know him, I realized we are not very compatible."

Jon smiled. "There's something I've been wanting to tell you for a little while," he stated and glanced down at his hands. "I didn't know what was going on with you and Andy, so I hesitated. When I saw him out tonight without you, I decided to jump at the chance."

"Okay," Chantal said, wondering if her curiosity was painted across her face.

Jon shifted in his seat and took a deep breath. "Chantal, I pray a lot, and well, I've been learning how to hear from God for as long as I can remember," he said. "I know God speaks to me by putting a desire in my heart, confirming it in His word, and then opening the door of opportunity. It just gets scary when I'm not sure if the door is open or not. Sometimes He unlocks the door but asks me to turn the knob."

Chantal raised her eyebrows in a questioning manner.

"So, basically, I've been praying about you," Jon stated hesitantly.

Chantal dropped her jaw. "Me?"

Jon nodded. "There is something about you that caught my attention," he said. "I don't know what it is, but whatever it is, it made me pray about you."

Chantal widened her eyes and swallowed deeply.

"I really like you," he admitted, looking at Chantal for only a few seconds before dropping his brown eyes to the table.

Chantal's heart fluttered. A warm vibe of joy shot through her limbs. *Is this really happening?*

"And…actually…I think that God might, um, have a plan for us," Jon stammered and then glanced up at Chantal.

I must be bright red, she thought.

Jon let out a nervous laugh. "Okay, you've got to help me out here," he said and looked her in the eye. "I have no idea what you even think of me."

Chantal looked away from him and smiled.

"Okay, a smile; that's good," Jon concluded.

Chantal nodded. "Yeah, smiles are usually good," she said and laughed nervously. "Sorry, you make me kind of nervous."

Jon smirked. "*I* make *you* nervous?"

Chantal nodded. "I don't really know what to say," she said, finding it difficult to make eye contact with him.

Jon shrugged slightly. "Just be honest. Do you have any interest in me?"

Chantal nodded and smiled bashfully.

"Really?!"

"Actually, I've been praying about you, too," she admitted.

"Really?!" Jon repeated.

"Really."

"Do you think God wants us to get closer?" Jon asked. He looked awestruck.

Chantal felt her face grow flush. "I think so," she replied. "If we both have been praying about it, and if we both want it, then it seems like we are having this conversation for a reason."

"This is awesome!" Jon exclaimed and jumped up from his seat.

Chantal laughed and stood up beside him.

"Can I hug you?" Jon asked.

Chantal could not remember a time when she felt more bashful. She smiled as Jon threw his arms around her. He hugged her so tightly that her feet lifted off the floor.

"This is one of the best moments of my life," Jon said softly. "Wow, you have no idea how many times I have played out this scenario in my head. This has turned out so much better than I even imagined. All of my friends have hooked up with girls, but I always believed that if I waited, then God would point me to someone I could cherish. Chantal, you are the most beautiful girl I have ever met. I am going to pray every day that God directs us in our friendship and helps us treat each other right."

"I will, too," Chantal said.

Jon wrapped his arms around Chantal again and hugged her tightly. A tingly sensation rushed through Chantal's body as she leaned into his embrace.

Is it possible to know at such a young age who I will spend the rest of my life loving? Am I naïve to think Jon will penetrate my heart like no other? Or to think he will mean anything to me by the start of high school? As she rested her head against his shoulder, she thanked God for being so gracious. She knew whatever God had planned for Jon and her would be endurable, because "a person standing alone can be attacked and defeated, but two can stand back-to-back and conquer." - Ecclesiastes 4:12

CHAPTER 35

Present Day

While reflecting on the events of seventh grade, Chantal could not help but become emotional. *Jon and I had meant so well,* she thought. *How did we let anything come between us? He loved me so much. He was so strong in his faith—what a beautiful person. I am so thankful that he reconciled with God last month. Every day, he seems more and more like the faithful kid I fell in love with years ago.* Chantal turned to a blank page in her seventh grade journal and began writing:

It is amazing what can happen in two years. People can change so much. I suppose if Jon had never begun partying with his friends, then I never would have given Andy a second chance. Perhaps it was all meant to be. If I hadn't given Andy a second chance, then maybe he never would have put his faith in Christ.

Jon learned a lot from our breakup, too, and he eventually found his way back to God. To this day I wonder if Cathy really did like Jon in seventh grade and if she plotted our breakup out of sheer jealousy. Maybe she got mad at God for Jon liking me? Maybe that was why she turned away from everyone and everything linked to the entire situation? Or maybe I'll just never understand her...

but it breaks my heart to see her so lost...she used to have such strong convictions. Thinking of how innocent she was in seventh grade makes me so sad.

What makes me happy is the positive change that I have seen in Chris. I am just so glad that Jon's prayers were answered and that Chris found freedom from his addictions. I hope with all of my heart that Jason will be the next one to get help. And then maybe he will find a way to help Cathy. Anything is possible.

***

After school the next day, Chantal arrived at the hospital with Jon, Lisa, and Leslie to see Katherine and Bobby sitting beside Andy's bed. Bobby barely glanced up at them when they entered the room. Katherine was holding Bobby's hand and gazing at him sympathetically. Chantal could tell from Bobby's expression that he was losing hope.

God had given Chantal confirmation and encouragement that everything was going to turn out fine. How could she share that with Bobby? Seeing the pain in his eyes made her wish she could trade places with him to give him some of her faith. No one in the room besides Jon would have been open to hearing about God. Even though Leslie was Protestant, and Katherine and Bobby were Catholic, they never seemed to like it when Chantal mentioned Jesus.

Chantal knew Andy's friends thought she was weird. She realized that Andy's desire for popularity kept him from wholeheartedly walking with God. Andy often agreed with agnostic views just to blend in with the crowd. He was lukewarm, with one foot in and one foot out of the church. He had just enough of God to relate to Chantal and just enough of the world to appear impartial. Chantal knew Andy's position was a horrible place to be. He was neither here nor there.

When Andy was away from his friends, he was a completely different person. He wanted to hear about what God was doing in Chantal's life. He wanted to pray with her. Sometimes, he would even email her scripture. As Chantal stared at Andy's blank face, she thought, *who are you?* With her whole heart, she wanted to believe that the side of Andy she saw when they were alone was the real Andy. She wanted to believe that who he was around his friends was a just a front.

138

Chantal knew one of Satan's tactics was to make people believe they could remain impartial and not face judgment. It was a great lie of his; it kept people from realizing that they were part of his kingdom. In truth, anyone who wasn't walking in the light was, in fact, walking in darkness. Chantal glanced around the room at Andy's friends, wondering if they would ever understand that.

After a moment, Chantal walked over to Andy's bed and affectionately touched his face. How had she allowed herself to fall in love with a stumbling block? Chantal wanted Andy to wake up as much as anyone else did. She missed her boyfriend terribly, but their month apart had been a blessing for Chantal in many ways. She had realized how much Andy held her back from her faith. While Andy was in a coma, Chantal realized that he was not the spiritual leader she desired to have as a boyfriend.

Previously, she had thought dating a Christian was all that mattered. She had not realized two believers could be on completely different paths. Although Chantal had never seen two unequally yoked animals try to carry a heavy load, she could imagine the difficultly. Two animals tied together, running in opposite directions, were not going to get anywhere. She had feared for quite some time that God was trying to show her that she and Andy were those two animals. Ignoring that revelation had become a heavy burden on Chantal's heart.

Chantal had talked to Jon about her situation with Andy. She admitted that while most people were praying for Andy to wake up healthy, she had also been praying for God to reveal to him the lukewarm temperature of his heart. It had been somewhat awkward for Chantal to confide in Jon about her relationship with Andy, but she knew Jon would give her Godly advice. Even though he had fallen off the straight and narrow path for a while, Jon was once again walking in the light.

Jon's advice had been simple, but it was more valuable than a book's worth of worldly advice. "Chantal, maybe God has taken Andy away for a little while to ease the pain of a future breakup. You've already suffered through the separation anxiety, and you are used to him not being around. If you feel like Andy is holding you back from furthering your walk with God, then you are unequally yoked. Jesus said, 'My burden is light.' If your relationship with Andy has become a heavy burden, then it is not of the Lord."

Jon's advice confirmed what Chantal already knew. She glanced down at Andy, praying for God to work a miracle in his heart.

Chantal loved Andy, and she hated the idea of breaking up with him. She knelt down by Andy's side, took ahold of his hand, and closed her eyes. Tears began streaming down her face as she prayed silently for their relationship.

"Chantal! Why can't I see you?" a faint voice called out, interrupting her prayer. Chantal shot her eyes open and planted them on Andy.

Leslie, Bobby, Katherine, Jon, and Lisa rushed to Andy's bedside.

"Did he just say something?" Katherine asked as she glanced from Andy to Chantal.

"He said he couldn't see me," Chantal replied, feeling her heart pound against her chest. "He said my name. Oh my gosh! He said my name! He remembered my name!"

"That's a really good sign," Leslie said.

"Should we go get the doctor?" Lisa asked.

"He must be dreaming about you," Bobby said.

Chantal smiled at Bobby, silently thanking God for Andy's sign of improvement. When she turned back to Andy, butterflies began fluttering around in her stomach. Andy began creasing his eyelids open. Once his eyes were open, he locked them on Chantal.

"Now I see you," he said quietly. Then he closed his eyes a second later and spread a peaceful smile across his lips.

OTHER BOOKS BY STACY A. PADULA

Gripped Part 3: The Fallout

Eighteen-year-old Marc Dunkin has received word from a detective that his oldest brother Taylor is a person of interest in a highly confidential case headed by the Boston Police Department. They know Taylor's clean; they know he wants out of the game; and they want to help make that happen. However, their "help" will come at a cost—one that may put Taylor and his entire family in grave danger.

Twenty-three-year-old Taylor Dunkin is trying to get his life back in order after an opiate addiction wreaked havoc on his once promising athletic future. Getting clean was a difficult feat, but breaking free from the Bilotti crime ring will present an even greater challenge.

Gripped Part 4: Smoke & Mirrors

After spending her first month of high school grounded, Cathy Kagelli is finally allowed to socialize and uncover what her boyfriend, Jason Davids, has been up to without her. When Cathy realizes Jason has been experimenting with a variety of drugs, she devises a plan to save him from himself... but she just may lose herself in the process.

Meanwhile Taylor Dunkin finds himself playing a game with even higher stakes because his life, his reputation, and the safety of everyone he loves are all on the line. Taylor's two younger brothers, Jordan and Marc, have been at odds for years, but they are brought together to decipher the mysterious clues Taylor is leaving regarding his whereabouts. As secrets are revealed, the Dunkin boys' relationships will be changed forever. In Taylor's weakest moment, he made a deal with the devil, and now there is a reckoning. But who will pay the price?

Gripped Part 5: Taylor's Story

Taylor Dunkin is missing.

The last message Jordan Dunkin receives from Taylor leads him to Taylor's abandoned Jeep. Each of Taylor's family members holds a piece of the puzzle, and as the Dunkins begin putting the details together, they are awakened to the possibility they may never see Taylor again.

No one can find Missy Kent.

Missy's boyfriend Luke Davids last saw her dancing with their friends at a nightclub, but she hasn't responded to anyone's texts or calls for hours.

Everything is connected.

Taylor and Missy's friends are dangerously close to learning the truth, but their ignorance might be the only thing keeping them safe. Every clue is leading them closer to peril.

The fifth book in the Gripped series moves through details at a thrilling pace. Secrets are revealed and lives are at stake. Taylor, Missy, their friends, and their families must figure out who they can trust before it's too late.

Montgomery Lake High #1: The Right Person

Growing up in the shadow of two NFL-destined cousins, Chris Dunkin has high hopes for his own future in football. However, a drug addiction threatens to destroy everything he has worked hard to attain. When Chris meets Courtney Angeletti—the mayor's straightedge Christian daughter—he believes she could be the source of inspiration he needs to overcome his destructive lifestyle. Courtney, however, has other ideas.

The desire to rebel has been tugging on Courtney's heartstrings for some time, and Chris's "bad-boy" reputation draws her to him like a moth to a flame. After all, he is a central part of the most popular clique in her high school. Will Chris pull Courtney away from her faith or will Courtney inspire him to overcome his rebellious lifestyle?

Montgomery Lake High #2: When Darkness Tries to Hide

Students at Montgomery Lake High believe the ominous clouds and impending storm will only bring a temporary interruption to their regularly scheduled lives. However, when the tempest grows worse and a classmate's life hangs in the balance, students must pull together to support each other and seek help for their friend. As the lines between cliques dissolve, dark secrets are revealed and hearts are transformed.

Montgomery Lake High #3: The Aftermath

At age fifteen, Jason Davids appears to have it all: high grades, popular friends, a beautiful girlfriend, and nearly any worldly thing that promises enjoyment at his disposal. Despite this, there is a persistent emptiness inside his heart. After failing to fill the void with achievements, relationships, and illicit substances, Jason finds himself intrigued by Jessie: a rather quiet girl, who is the daughter of a local pastor. How is it possible that she stands for everything his lifestyle opposes yet possesses the one thing he has been searching for all along?

Montgomery Lake High #5: The Forces Within

After being trapped inside his own body, unable to communicate with anyone but his own thoughts, Andy Rosetti finally wakes up from the coma that controlled his life for one month. But upon awakening, Andy finds himself and his friends in an unfamiliar setting: a mansion riddled with secret passages and supernatural forces. As his friends fall prey to the entities surrounding them, Andy must figure out if the darkness lies within the mansion's walls or within the people surrounding him.

ABOUT THE AUTHOR

Stacy A. Padula grew up in Pembroke, Massachusetts. She is the founder of Briley & Baxter Publications, the founder of South Shore College Consulting & Tutoring, a co-founder of BLE Pictures, and the author of thirteen books. She began writing her first book series, *Montgomery Lake High*, when she was a teenager because she saw a need for realistic Y.A. books that address topics such as substance abuse and bullying. Between 2010-2014 all five *Montgomery Lake High* books were published. In 2017, she began writing her second series, *Gripped*, which serves as both a prequel and sequel to her first series. *Gripped* parts 1-5 were published between 2019-2021. She is currently writing part 6. In 2019, she also wrote her first screenplay, an adaptation of her novel *The Aftermath*, and worked on writing a pilot for *Gripped*, which caught the attention of Hollywood producers.

In 2020, she began writing a third book series with NBA Coach Brett Gunning. Geared towards children ages three through eight, Stacy and Brett's *On The Right Path* book series has been endorsed by Joel Osteen, Mike D'Antoni, and Kevin McHale as a series that belongs in every school, library, and household. Both Stacy's Gripped series and On the Right Path series are currently being adapted for TV by Emmy award-winning producer Mark Blutman.

Stacy has been featured in Marquis Who's Who in America (2018-Present) for excellence in literature and education, Marquis Who's Who in the World (2018-Present), and Cambridge Who's Who for Young Professionals (2009). In 2018, she was awarded the Albert Nelson Lifetime Achievement Award, and in 2019, the International Association of Top Professionals (IAOTP of New York, NY) chose Stacy as its "Top Educational Consultant of the Year."

In 2020, she was named "Empowered Woman of the Year" by IAOTP and a "Social Impact Hero" by Authority Magazine for her support of animal rescues through her publishing company. She was also chosen to be on the cover of T.I.P. Magazine, an international business publication.

In June of 2021, Stacy was featured on the famous Reuters Building in Times Square as Empowered Woman of the Year. In 2022, she was named "Top Inspirational Author of the Year" and was honored at a gala at the Bellagio in Las Vegas in December. She was also broadcast for her award on the Planet Hollywood Jumbotron overlooking the Las Vegas Strip. Her novel *Gripped Part 5: Taylor's Story* won the Silver Award and *Gripped Part 1: The Truth We Never Told* won the Gold Award for "Best Teen Book" in the 2022 Readers' Choice Awards.

For 2023, Stacy has been named "Top Global Impact Author of the Year" for her literary work on several continents, and she will be honored at a gala at The Plaza in New York City. In addition, she was chosen to be featured in an international publication titled 50 Fearless Leaders for 2023. She also was asked to serve as a judge for the Scholastic Art & Writing Awards, the nation's oldest and most prestigious contest for creative young adults, sponsored by Bloomberg Philanthropies, The New York Times, and Scholastic.

CONNECT WITH US!

Gripped Book Series Instagram @gripped.book.series
Stacy's Instagram @author_stacypadula
Stacy's Twitter @MLHBookSeries
Cathy's Instagram @ckagelli99
Chantal's Instagram @chantal_kagelli
Jason's Instagram @jds_on
Lisa's Instagram @lisa_ankerman99
Chris's Instagram @dunkin_85
Luke's Instagram @lukedavids97
Alyssa's Instagram @alyssa_kelly02
www.stacyapadula.com
www.brileybaxterbooks.com
www.highambition.org

DID YOU ENJOY

MLH #4?

If you loved this book, would you leave a review on Amazon?

www.ingramcontent.com/pod-product-compliance
Lightning Source LLC
Chambersburg PA
CBHW071528100726
47908CB00004B/1328